MAYHEM ON
MACKINAC ISLAND

An AudioCraft Publishing, Inc. book

This book is a work of fiction. Names, places, characters and incidents are used fictitiously, or are products of the author's very active imagination.

Michigan Chillers #1: Mayhem on Mackinac Island
ISBN 1-893699-05-6

Librarians/media specialists:
PCIP/MARC records available at www.americanchillers.com

Cover Illustrations by Dwayne Harris
Cover layout and design by Sue Harring

Printed in USA

Johnathan Rand's
MICHIGAN CHILLERS

#1: Mayhem on Mackinac Island

VISIT THE OFFICIAL WORLD HEADQUARTERS OF AMERICAN CHILLERS & MICHIGAN CHILLERS!

The all-new HOME for books by Johnathan Rand! Featuring books, hats, shirts, bookmarks and other cool stuff not available anywhere else in the world! Plus, watch the American Chillers website for news of special events and signings at *CHILLERMANIA* with author Johnathan Rand! Located in northern lower Michigan, on I-75 just off exit 313!

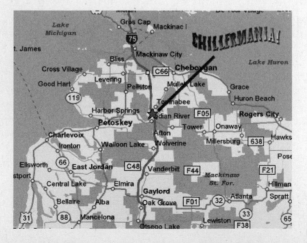

OPENING OCTOBER, 2005!

www.americanchillers.com

1

My name is Sandy, and I'm twelve. Sandra Jean Johnson, if you're really mad at me. But usually everybody calls me Sandy, except my brother Tim. He calls me a lot of other dumb names . . . names that he makes up, mostly. Silly names . . . like *Sandy-Pandy* and *Sandra Jean, the Queen of Mean*. Which isn't fair, because I'm not mean. And he calls me *Munchkin*. I hate that one the worst. It even *sounds* bad.

Munchkin.

I'm a year older than he is, but I'm about an inch shorter. Just because of that, he calls me Munchkin.

I hate being called that.

I have sandy-blonde hair that fits my name perfectly. It's just past my shoulders.

Once I got it cut real short, but I didn't like it. Now I wear it long, sometimes in a pony-tail or a French braid. Tim has hair a little darker than mine, only his is a lot shorter.

Of all the seasons, I like summer the best. We live in Birmingham, Michigan, but we spend the whole summer on Mackinac Island. It's about a five hour drive from our house in Birmingham.

Mackinac Island is an island in Lake Huron, which is one of the Great Lakes. Actually, in my opinion, it's bigger than a Great Lake. It's HUGE! Much bigger than any lake I've ever seen. It's so blue and beautiful that sometimes I never want to leave. There are lots of trees on the island, and I meet lots of cool new friends every summer. Every summer we have a blast.

Except for *this* summer.

This summer turned into a horrible nightmare—worse than I could have ever imagined.

But first, I guess I have to tell you about what went on *last* summer. That's when something really weird happened.

Tim and I were at our Uncle Jerry's house . . . that's the house we stay at on Mackinac Island. Mom and dad and Tim and I stay with Uncle Jerry and Aunt Ruth. We stay from June all the way till school starts. It's so much fun! Aunt Ruth and Uncle Jerry are really nice. Their house is really big and pretty and it's right near the water. They have a dock that extends way out over the lake. There's even a diving board there! We swim a lot and go for boat rides.

I asked Dad one day if I could ride my bike all the way around the paved footpath that goes around the island. It's a long way . . . like eight miles or something.

"Okay," Dad told me. "But Tim has to go with you."

"Great," I whispered, rolling my eyes. I did NOT want Tim to go with me!

Tim was in his bedroom playing his Game Boy, but he heard us talking. "Hey, that sounds like fun!" he yelled. He ran into the living room where I was. "Let's go Munchkin!" he said.

Terrific.

"Come on, slow poke!" he said, running out the door. He already had his helmet on!

I wish I could do some things all by myself once in a while.

But something was about to happen on the bike trip that made me glad that we were together. REALLY glad.

2

My bike is red. Tim's is blue. They're mountain bikes . . . we each got one for Christmas that year. Before that, we rented bikes from a store on the island.

Anyway, we peddled through downtown. I LOVE downtown Mackinac Island! They don't allow cars on the island—anywhere! We can ride our bikes in the middle of the street if we want to.

But—

You have to watch out! There are lots of other people on bikes and even more people walking . . . but the thing you really have to watch out for is the horses! On Mackinac Island, horses are used to pull carriages and wagons! Since there are no cars, horses pull buggies around the island. The buggies and carriages carry everything from luggage to supplies to people. You can even go for a tour on a horse drawn carriage if you want.

But the best thing about downtown is the delicious aroma of sweet, tantalizing fudge! It's everywhere—drifting out from the stores, through open doors and windows—yum! I could eat fudge all day.

You probably could, too, if you stayed on Mackinac Island all summer.

"Watch out!" I suddenly yelled at Tim. He wasn't watching where he was going and he almost ran into a man pushing a cart! Tim swerved just in time. That was a close one.

We rode through town and continued on the paved blacktop path that winds all around the island. It's a fun ride. You can see boats on the water, and even the Michigan mainland in the distance. And seagulls! There are lots of seagulls whirling above and sitting near the shore.

When we were about halfway around the island, Tim stopped. "I'm tired," he said. "I need to rest." He hopped off and laid his bike against a tree. He took his helmet off and set it on his bike seat.

For the first time in my life, I think I actually agreed with him. I was tired, too.

I hopped off my bike and walked down to the water where Tim was. He was skipping rocks.

I picked up a nice flat rock and let it fly. It

skipped fifteen times!

"Showoff!" Tim said. But he was just jealous. He knew he couldn't skip a rock fifteen times if he tried! I felt proud.

Suddenly, he turned and pointed. "Look at that!" he said.

I turned and I couldn't believe what I saw. I mean . . . I just couldn't! I had to get closer and get a better look.

And THAT'S what got us into trouble.

3

It was a man! A very small man, sitting in a great big tree. He had long gray hair that flowed over his shoulders and a long gray beard. And a tall, funny hat that was cone-shaped. The hat had silver and gold stars all over it. He was wearing a long white robe. Boy! Did he look out of place on Mackinac Island, not to mention the fact that he was sitting in a tree! He looked like he was a magician or something.

The tree he was sitting in was really old looking. It had a lot of long, black spiny branches, like thin fingers, but no leaves. I was sure that the tree was dead.

"Hello!" Tim shouted. He said it so loud and unexpectedly that I jumped. I hate it when he does that.

The sound must have scared the man because all of a sudden he disappeared! I caught a flash of his white robe, and it looked like he just ran along the branch and into the tree!

Tim wanted to find out where he went. "Come on, Munchkin!" he said, running past our bikes and into the woods.

"Quit calling me Munchkin!" I scolded. But I followed him anyway.

The forest on the other side of the paved footpath was really thick. There was no trail so I had to use my arms to pull branches and limbs out of my way. It was so thick that it was hard to walk. Trees grew close together and there were vines and small branches everywhere.

I accidentally walked into a spider web and the thin gooey string stuck to my face. Pitooey! I hate spiders. I wiped the sticky web away with my hands and continued after Tim.

But there was something that was very strange.

We walked and walked, but we couldn't find the little old man! It was like he just disappeared completely. Weird.

Tim stopped beneath the old tree, looking up and around. "I wonder where he went," he said, gazing up into the branches. I stopped walking too.

I looked up, peering through the dense limbs

above, but I didn't see any sign of the man. I was really hoping I would be the first to see the tiny man again. Tim is always discovering new things first, but I wanted to be first this time.

The forest was very quiet. On Mackinac Island you obviously don't hear any cars, because there aren't any. Once in a while you hear a plane overhead. But all we could hear in the forest were birds. Birds and crickets.

"He couldn't just disappear into thin air," I said.

"Maybe he disappeared into fat air," Tim said, making fun of me.

"There's no such thing as fat air!" I said. But then again, maybe there was. I didn't know for sure.

We stared up into the trees for a few more seconds, but we didn't see any sign of the man with the white robe and funny hat.

"Let's go back," Tim said finally, taking one last look up into the trees. I followed his gaze and we squinted up into the sky.

No funny old man. He had disappeared.

I turned and started to walk back to the footpath. My feet crunched on sticks and branches.

"Aaahhhhhgggghh!!" someone screamed in terror, and I recognized the voice instantly.

That someone was Tim!

4

I stopped and spun around. Tim was staring at his feet. He was trying to walk, but he couldn't.

His feet were trapped in quicksand!

It was all the way up and over his ankles. Tim grabbed a branch and tried to pull himself out. He freed one foot but the other one kept getting sucked farther into the ground!

"Help me Munchkin!" he yelled. I would have been mad at him for calling me Munchkin, but I was too scared. Tim was in trouble, and I needed to help.

I walked toward him, watching the ground carefully. I didn't want to step into quicksand too!

I couldn't get real close to him because there was quicksand all around him. Dark, syrup-like mud was everywhere.

"Hurry!" Tim said. He was sinking faster, and the brown goo was almost up to his knee. He held his other leg up in the air as far as he could so it wouldn't get stuck again. If he wasn't in so much danger he would've looked very funny!

I searched around and found a long stick.

"Grab this!" I hollered, holding it out.

Tim grabbed it and I pulled with all my might. I'm not very big, but I'm really pretty strong. I think I'm even stronger than Tim.

I pulled and pulled like I never had before. I felt like I was in a game of tug-o-war . . . a *dangerous* game of tug-o-war . . . and if I didn't win, we were really going to be in trouble.

But I wasn't going to lose. I was sure of it. I kept pulling harder and harder on the branch.

"Hang on tight!" I told Tim. "Whatever you do, don't let go!"

Finally Tim's foot came free. He tumbled forward and I lost my balance, falling back. Tim landed on top of me.

"Get off me, you goof," I told him. But I really was glad that he was okay.

"That was close, Munch," he said.

Munch. I think that's worse than being called Munchkin.

He stood up, looking at his leg. His sneaker and the leg of his pants were covered with brown gunk all the way up to his knee.

"Mom's gonna freak out," he said. But I know he was really glad that he got out of the quicksand. If he had been stuck for just a few more seconds, there's no telling what would have happened.

But all of this happened last summer.

What happened this summer was worse.

FAR worse.

5

Tim and I were riding our bikes around town, but it started raining so we hung out downtown for awhile. I went into the Island Bookstore and Tim went into the toy store. We both went into a couple of fudge shops, and I bought a big chunk of fudge called 'Moose Tracks'. Yum!

Finally the rain stopped and we got on our bikes again. We rode by the marina, and past the big white fort on the hill. The Governor of Michigan even has a summer home on Mackinac Island, and we rode past it, too.

There were a lot of people walking on the path, but the farther we got from town, the less people there were. Soon we didn't see anyone anymore.

By this time we had pretty much forgotten all about the old man and the tree and the quicksand.

So when I was riding past the spot where we had spotted the old man last year, I couldn't believe my eyes!

"Tim, look!" I shouted. Tim was in front of me riding his blue bike. He stopped and turned to see where I was pointing.

It was the same strange old man with the funny hat!

He was sitting in the same old tree in the same place where he had been last year. Same long, gray hair and beard. Same weird looking pointy hat with gold and silver stars. He wasn't more than fifty feet away from us.

"Hey!" Tim shouted. Sometimes when Tim says 'hey' what he really means is 'hello.'

I was sure the old man was going to run away, just like he did last year.

But he didn't.

In fact, the old man did just the opposite. He waved at us, urging us to come closer.

"Come on," Tim said, hopping off his bike.

"No, Tim," I said. "Let's stay here." But actually, I wanted to go see for myself, too.

"Oh, come on Munchkin," he whined.

"Remember what happened last year," I reminded him.

"Don't worry, I'll watch out," he replied,

referring to the quicksand.

I reluctantly followed him into the woods and looked up. To my surprise, the old man was still in the tree, smiling, still waving at us to come forward. I was walking slow, keeping a close watch on the ground. I sure didn't want to step in any quicksand!

When we got close to the tree we stopped, and guess what?

The old man had disappeared again!

So strange.

"Where in the world did he go?" Tim asked, staring up into the branches. I looked up into the tree, too . . . but I kept glancing down at the ground, expecting to see quicksand. I was relieved when I didn't see any.

"This is just like last year," I whispered. "He disappeared last year, too."

"Well, I'm *going* to go find him," Tim stated seriously. "People just don't *disappear*." He walked toward the trunk of the huge, dead tree and looked up.

"What are you *doing?!?*" I asked him. But I already knew.

Tim was going to climb the tree!

"No, Tim!" I told him. "I don't think it's a good idea."

And it wasn't a good idea. It wasn't a good idea at all, as we were about to find out.

6

The trunk of the old tree was really, really big. It was black and wrinkled with age. Branches grew out from everywhere, going way up into the air. It looked bony and weird, like some old black skeleton. It was kind of spooky looking.

Tim grabbed a low branch and pulled himself up into the tree. I still didn't think it was a good idea, but I didn't say anything more. Tim hardly ever listens to me anyway. If you have a brother, I'm sure you know what it's like sometimes.

"Be careful," was all I said.

"Quit telling me what to do," he said sternly. "You're not Mom."

"No, I'm not, but I'm older than you and you have to listen to me."

"I do not. I'm bigger than you, Munchkin."

"By one inch! And I'm not a Munchkin! Quit calling me that!"

Sometimes I just can *not* stand Tim.

I watched him pull himself up onto a branch, thinking to myself that if he fell, Mom was going to blame *me* for not keeping him out of the tree. Then, not only would Tim be hurt, but it would be *my* fault!

Sometimes it's hard being an older sister.

I was watching Tim carefully, watching his every move as he reached for branches and pulled himself up through the tree. He's actually a very good tree climber. He can climb trees like a chimpanzee. But I couldn't help being a wee bit nervous.

He looped his arm around a big fat branch and pulled himself higher still. He was already twenty feet off the ground!

Just be careful, Tim, I thought. *Just be careful.*

A motion out of the corner of my eye caught my attention.

A branch had moved all by itself!

I couldn't believe it. A branch started moving, curling in like a long, skinny finger. Then another branch started to move. Then another.

The tree had come alive!

"Tim!" I yelled. *"Look out!"* But he was already too far up into the tree to hear me. I watched

in horror as the branches slithered about, twisting and turning like black snakes in the sky above. It was the most bizarre thing I had ever seen.

I wanted to run, but I think I was too afraid to! And I couldn't leave Tim. I didn't know what to do.

All of a sudden a long branch shot through the air, heading right for Tim!

7

"WATCH OUT!" I screamed at the top of my lungs.

But it was too late. Tim didn't even see the branch coming.

It wrapped itself around him like one of those snakes I've seen on TV. You know the kind . . . Boa Constrictors is what they're called. I've seen them on the Discovery channel. They wrap themselves tightly around their prey and squish them.

That's just what this branch looked like it was going to do!

The branch wrapped around Tim, and then another branch did the same.

"HELP!!!" Tim screamed. The branch pulled him away from the tree and held him suspended in the air. Now I was more than just scared. I was

horrified. I was so horrified that I didn't even see the branch that sneaked up behind me!

It grabbed me without warning, wrapping its wrinkled arm around my waist, holding me tight. I screamed and grabbed at the branch. I tried to pull it away, but it held fast. I tried to hit it with my fist, but that didn't help at all.

Then it lifted me off the ground!

I was pulled high up into the air, higher, until I was only a few feet from Tim. We were both struggling to get free. Problem was, if we did break away, we would fall fifty feet to the ground!

"Let go of me!" I screamed, trying to pry the branches from around my waist. "Let me go!!"

Mom and Dad are not going to like this, I thought. *Mom and Dad are not going to like this one bit.*

Tim and I were both screaming and yelling, hoping someone would hear. We were both frantically trying to pull the wiry branches from around us.

Suddenly I heard voices. People!

I was way up in the air, and I could see everything—the lake, the bike path—and two people on their bicycles! They were riding on the thin black strip of blacktop that wound around the island.

"Help!" Tim and I both screamed. "Help! Help us!"

But it was as if the people couldn't hear us!

They just kept riding along, taking their time on the bike path, talking to each other. In a few seconds they disappeared from sight.

"Tim, what are we going to do?!?!" I screamed. But Tim couldn't hear me. He was too busy struggling to release himself from the clutches of the branches.

Then we were moving. The branches began pulling us inward, toward the tree trunk!

I kept struggling, trying to wrestle from the squeezing branch, but it was no use. We couldn't get away.

The tree kept pulling us inward, closer, closer to the trunk . . . .

And suddenly I realized what was going to happen . . . and it almost scared me to death.

8

The tree branches still held us tight, but now Tim and I were being pulled toward a huge hole that had opened up in the trunk! It was like some big, dark mouth. I could almost hear the tree licking its lips in bloodthirsty anticipation.

"Sandy!" Tim screamed. *"Help me! Help me, Sandy!"*

Tim RARELY calls me Sandy.

But there was nothing I could do. I had my own problems. I was bound by wiry limbs that were wrapped tightly around my torso.

If only Tim hadn't decided to chase after that funny little man!

The mouth in the tree opened wider and Tim was first.

"Noooooooo!!!!" he screamed, as he was forced into the hungry mouth of the tree. *"Sandy! Help meeeeee!!!!"*

And then, in the blink of an eye, Tim was gone. He had been swallowed up by the tree.

Now I was REALLY scared. I was scared because Tim had been devoured by a tree . . . but I was also scared because the tree branch that was carrying me was now pulling me toward the gaping mouth.

I was going to be next!

I tried kicking at the tree with my feet, but it didn't help. I was being pulled closer . . . closer . . . closer still.

And then everything was black. The branch released its grip and I was free, but that didn't matter now. I had just been eaten! I had been gobbled up by the tree!

It was dark and I could feel the hard wood of the tree all around me.

Oh no, I thought. *Oh no, this is it. This is IT!*

Then I could hear Tim!

"Sandy!" he was yelling! *"Sandy, can you hear me?!?!?"*

"*Yes!*" I shouted, but I still couldn't see him. He sounded very far away.

I was being pulled farther into the tree, but now the wood seemed to be getting softer, and it wasn't crushing me. I struggled to see, to find a way out, but there was none. I was trapped for good.

Then all of a sudden I bumped into something soft, and I jumped and screamed.

It was Tim!

"Sandy . . . is that you?!?!?!" he said.

"Of course it's me!" I said. I don't think I have ever been so happy to hear his voice.

Then a very strange thing happened. (As if being eaten by a tree isn't strange enough!)

I could feel myself being suspended in the air. It was like both Tim and I were weightless. It was dark and black and we couldn't see anything. I thought that this must be how it feels to be an astronaut in space.

"What's going on?" Tim asked, his voice shaking.

"I don't know," I replied.

I tried to move and suddenly I realized that I could walk. The ground beneath my feet felt soft and squishy, like thick moss.

I took a step forward and bumped into something hard.

"Ouch!" I said. Tim held on to my hand and now he took a step in my direction. It was still darker than night and I couldn't see him. I've never been anywhere that was so dark.

I ran my hands on the hard wall in front of me. It was rough like wood, so I thought that we must somehow still be inside the tree.

"Where are we?" Tim asked.

Right. Like I was going to be able to answer *that* question.

I continued moving my hands along the wall.

Suddenly I felt something.

It was like a crevice, a crack of some kind. I pushed my fingers into the split, trying to pull.

I saw light!

As I pulled the crack apart with my fingers, daylight started to shine through!

"Tim! Help me! This might be a way out!"

Tim drew closer to my side and he placed his hands in the crack that was opening up.

"Harder!" I told him. The space got wider, and more light came in.

"We can do it!" I told him. "We just . . . have . . . to . . . pull . . . harder . . . ." It was a struggle to speak because I was pulling so hard.

Finally, we got it open far enough so that we could slip through. I wasted no time, and Tim didn't either. He held on to the belt loop of my jeans to make sure that I wasn't going to leave him.

We both tumbled into the light and looked around in amazement.

The world we had left was gone, and the world around us was nothing like I have ever seen before in my life.

9

"Wow."

It was all I could say. Tim couldn't say anything. We both just stared.

There were trees that grew so high into the sky they disappeared into the air. Their trunks were as big around as a house. I remember seeing big Redwood trees once when we went to California. That's what these trees looked like, except the trunks were *blue!* The tree trunks were blue and, high above, way up in the sky, the leaves were red.

And the entire forest was that way. Small bushes had yellow limbs and purple leaves. The grass beneath our feet was green, but it was a very shiny, emerald green.

It was very quiet, except for a small, unseen

creek that was babbling nearby. There were no birds, no crickets. No cars or planes. No people.

"This is really weird," Tim said.

Finally I turned and looked at where we had come from. It was just as I had suspected: we had emerged from one of the enormous trees. As crazy as it sounds, we had been pulled into a tree by the tree itself . . . only now we were somewhere totally different. I was sure that we weren't on Mackinac Island anymore!

My friends at school would NEVER believe this.

"How do we get out of here?" Tim said. But I didn't know. I thought that maybe if we climbed back inside the tree we could somehow climb back out, but I wasn't sure if I wanted to do that.

All of a sudden the hole in the tree where we had came from began to close. There was a crunching sound as the crack pulled together.

Wherever we were, we were stuck there.

I don't know if you've ever had the feeling that you were all alone, on your own, but let me tell you, it is NOT fun. I felt like I was going to cry, but I didn't. I think Tim did, just a tiny bit, but I didn't say anything.

We were alone. Completely alone.

I don't know how long we just stood there like that, staring. Everything looked so weird!

Tim suddenly spoke and raised his arm,

pointing. "Sandy . . . *look.*"

I looked where he was pointing and I saw a flash of movement by one of the huge tree trunks.

Now I was REALLY scared.

Before I was scared because we were all alone.

Now I was scared because I realized that we were in a strange world that I had never seen before.

I was scared because we *weren't* alone.

There was someone . . . or *something* . . . else here, too.

10

There comes a time when you stop worrying about being late for supper and just worry about the problem at hand.

That time was now.

We saw a movement again, this time in some bushes.

"What do you think it is?" I whispered.

Tim took a step closer to me. He was scared, too. "I don't know," he stammered.

The bushes moved again.

"Maybe it's that little man with the long hair and the pointy hat," I said.

"RIGHTY-HO, RIGHTY-HO," a voice suddenly boomed out. He must have heard me! His voice scared me, and Tim jumped too.

Suddenly the little man appeared from the bushes!

I grabbed Tim and he grabbed me and held on tight. I wanted to run, fast and furious, but then what? Where would I go?

The man actually wasn't so little after all. I mean, he was little as far as a man was concerned. He was about my height, but his pointed hat made him look taller. His long gray hair fell over his shoulders and his beard went all the way down to his waist! His white robe almost touched the ground.

As he drew closer I could feel Tim hold me tighter. He was REALLY scared. So was I.

"Yes, indeed," the old man said again. "It is I, the only—"

His beard suddenly caught on a small branch! It yanked his head around and he yelled.

"Owww!!" he shouted. "I *hate* it when that happens!"

If I hadn't been so afraid I might have thought that it was very funny.

He untangled his beard from the branch and kept walking toward us. I guess he didn't look real scary, but I was afraid anyway. Being in such a strange, unknown place can be a pretty scary thing sometimes.

"What . . . what do you want?" I stammered. I think Tim was too afraid to say anything.

But the man ignored me! Instead, he just kept

looking at me, then at Tim, then at me. He glared at us with wide, silver-blue eyes.

"Yes, yes," he said. "I think you'll do. You both look healthy. Healthy and strong enough. You'll work out *perfect.*"

"Perfect for . . . for *what?*" Tim sputtered. He was still scared, but he wasn't holding me so tight anymore.

"To find the Key, of course!" the old man replied quickly, throwing up his hands like we were supposed to know what he was talking about.

"What key?" I asked.

Again, he looked perplexed. "*The* Key," he said. Then: "The Stone Key. It's the key I need to get out of this infernal place."

"Well, uh . . . Mr., uh—" I began. But I didn't know what to call him. I think he sensed this, because he interrupted.

"I am The Great Salami Knockingbuck Mortimer Jeremiah Tuttworth," he replied proudly.

Now I did laugh!

"The Great *what?*" Tim asked.

The old man repeated himself, and this time Tim and I both laughed.

The old man looked at us coldly. I hope we didn't make him mad.

"I'm sorry, Mister—uh . . . Great . . .uh . . . sir . . . but that's such a strange name."

"And tell me, young one, just what is *your*

45

name?"

"I'm Sandy. Sandy Johnson. This is my brother Tim."

Suddenly the man let out a roaring laugh that thundered through the forest!

"Those are the FUNNIEST names I've ever—"

His voice was suddenly interrupted by a terrible whooshing sound, like large flapping wings! A long shadow came over the forest, and the entire woods went almost completely dark.

"Oh no!" the old man cried. "It's a Wartwing! Follow me! We must take cover!"

A what?!?! I thought. I had never heard of a Wartwing before. I didn't know what one was.

And I'm not sure I really wanted to.

I was frightened, but I had to look up to see what had scared the old man so much.

I was immediately sorry that I did. What I saw above us was the scariest thing I had ever seen in my life.

It was a creature. It had giant wings like a bird, but it was all brown and had scales like a dragon. And warts like a toad! Its mouth was open and I could see a long red tongue lashing from side to side.

It was as big as a house—and it was coming right for us!

Have you ever been so scared that you just couldn't move? That's how I felt! I just stood there, looking up into the sky as this horrible creature swooped closer.

"Run! Now!" I heard the man with the pointed hat yell. "Run now, or we're all doomed!"

That was all the prodding I needed. I sprang forward, following the old man as he ran through the strange, colorful forest. Tim was at my side. We ran as fast as we could, following the old man over the shiny green grass as he led us deeper into the forest.

I could hear the shrieking cries of the Wartwing behind and above us. I could even hear the thunderous pumping of its wings as they beat the air.

Tim managed a quick glance over his shoulder.

"Sandy! Now there's TWO of them!"

There's a time when you just trust your brother and you don't need to see for yourself. Not often, but I took his word for it this time. If Tim said that there were two creatures, I believed him.

"Hurry!" the old man yelled, turning his head back toward us as he shouted. "If we don't hurry, there'll be more! Then there will be no escape!"

Suddenly, I saw the old man's white robe duck beneath some branches. Tim and I followed, not sure of where we were going. But at the moment, we didn't care. We just didn't want that huge Wartwing to catch us.

I think ANYTHING would be better than that!

As I ducked beneath the branches I stumbled and fell forward, crashing to the ground and rolling. Tim had tumbled as well, and I fell on top of him and we both rolled, arms and legs flailing. We came to a stop.

We were in a small room! It looked like we were on the inside of a tree, like the inside of a giant trunk.

The old man suddenly burst behind us, closing a heavy wood door. There was a long board that served as a bolt, and he slid it over the door.

"Whew," he said. "That was close."

My heart was pounding. I was out of breath,

48

and so was Tim.

"What was that . . . that *thing?*" I asked.

"A Wartwing. The ugliest, nastiest, meanest thing in the Captive Forest."

"The WHAT forest?" Tim asked.

The old man looked annoyed. "You sure ask a lot of questions," he said.

"Well, Mr. Great, uh, whatever you call yourself," I began to say. I was starting to get a little annoyed myself. I don't think Mom and Dad were going to like the fact that we were being chased by Wartwings. On Mackinac Island of all places.

Or . . . wherever we were.

"You may call me the Great Tuttworth for short," the old man began.

Fine. I could remember Great Tuttworth.

"We don't know where we are," I continued. "My brother and I were sucked into an old tree, and somehow we wound up here. I don't know where we are."

"You are presently in my home in the Captive Forest on the Isle of Mayhem."

"Isle of Mayhem!?!?" Tim and I both said in unison.

"Precisely," the Great Tuttworth answered, nodding his head. His long hat bowed forward as he nodded. "The Isle of Mayhem. Quite a dreadful place, really. I've been here, oh, probably about seven thousand years. Give or take several hundred."

"Seven thousand years!?!?!" I exclaimed. "What happened to Mackinac Island?!?!?!? The Fort! The Grand Hotel?!?!?"

The Great Tuttworth looked perplexed.

"I'm not sure I've heard of those places," he said. "But then again, I've been held prisoner in the Captive Forest so very, very long."

"But what do you want from us?" Tim asked.

"The Stone Key," the old man replied. "I must have the Stone Key. It is somewhere on this island."

"Can't you go get it?" I asked him.

Suddenly he looked very sad. "No, I'm afraid I can't," he answered. "You see, I was once a Miracle-Maker. The most powerful Miracle-Maker in the land. Many years ago, during the War of Magic, the terrible King Balderdash unleashed the powers of darkness on this island. It used to be called the Isle of Miracles. But ever since, it has become known as the Isle of Mayhem. I cannot leave the Captive Forest because of an invisible magical barrier all around it. I am stuck, I'm afraid, until I have the Stone Key. The Stone Key is the only hope for returning the Isle of Mayhem back to the Isle of Miracles. And it has even greater importance than that."

"What's that?" I asked. I was finding all of this very hard to believe.

"Because not only is it the key to unlocking

the Captive Forest," he explained, "But it is also the same very key that locks up all of the powers of darkness. When the Stone Key is found and the Captive Forest is unlocked, the Isle of Miracles will come back . . . and all of the powers of darkness will be cast into the Abyss of No Return."

Now I REALLY knew that Mom and Dad weren't going to believe this!

"The Stone Key is the only thing that can lock the powers of darkness away," the Great Tuttworth said sadly. He looked grim and almost helpless.

I suddenly felt very sorry for him. Away from his home and family for so long. He really did look very sad. And lonely.

"Where is the key?" I asked.

"It is buried deep within Skull Mountain, here on the Isle of Mayhem. I am trapped in this forest. I can't leave to find the key. That's why I must ask you to help me."

"What if we don't want to?" Tim asked. "I mean . . . you can't *make* us."

"I'm afraid you have no choice," the Miracle-Maker replied, shaking his head.

"What do you mean by that?" Tim asked. "I mean . . . we have to get home. Mom's making supper right now, and if we're late—"

"There won't be any supper for you at your home tonight," the Great Tuttworth interrupted.

He took a step towards us, staring coldly into

our eyes.

"You see, the same key that frees me from the Captive Forest is the same key that will open the Door of Realms that will take you back to your own world. If you do not find the Stone Key, it will be impossible for you to ever go home. *Ever.*"

This was crazy! The Isle of Mayhem? The Captive Forest . . . Skull Mountain . . . a Door of Realms? I knew right then that we were in deep trouble.

12

I guess what worried me the most was that mom and dad would be looking for us soon. When we didn't come home, I'm sure they would call the police. They'd have everybody searching for us. Then how would we explain it?

I mean, there's no way that they would believe that we were on some strange island looking for a key!

That is IF we made it home.

I guess if we wanted to see mom and dad and our friends again, we'd have to find the Stone Key.

"So, where do we look? How do we find it?" I asked.

The Great Tuttworth shook his head. His long, gray hair swished from side to side. "I'm afraid that is something even I do not know. I know that the key is somewhere deep inside Skull Mountain, and that is all."

There was that mountain again. Skull Mountain. I didn't even like the *sound* of it.

"But if there's a magical force around the forest, how do we get out?" Tim asked.

"The magical wall around the forest will not hurt you, nor will it keep you in or out. You can come and go as you wish."

"As long as those Wartwings don't get us," I said.

"Those nasty things," the Great Tuttworth replied. "They're all over the island. I'm afraid you'll have to watch out for them everywhere."

Great. We're going to be eaten by flying toads with wings.

He reached into a pocket in his robe and pulled out two stones. Each stone was light gray colored and had a strange carving inside it. He handed one to me. It had a dragonfly carved into it. Then he handed one to Tim. It had a spider carved into it.

"Be very careful not to lose these," he said. "They will help you a great deal." He looked at me and continued speaking. "*Your* stone will allow you to fly. Not very far and not for very long. It will never lose its power as long as you have it. If you lose it, the power will leave. You are the only person who will be able to use its special powers. That is so if it falls into the hands of someone bad, they can't use it.

"Your stone—" he looked at Tim— "your stone will allow you to climb anywhere. Rocks, trees . . . anything. You, too, must also be very careful not to lose your stone."

Tim looked at his stone and rolled it through his fingers. "But . . . but how do I use it?" he asked.

"It is very easy. Try and climb something. Right now. Go ahead. Try and climb the wall."

Tim looked at the Great Tuttworth like he was out of his mind!

"Go on," I said. "Try it, Tim."

Reluctantly, Tim walked over to a wall, unconvinced that a simple little stone was going to allow him to climb like a spider. He looked back at me, then at the Great Tuttworth.

"Try it," the Miracle-Maker urged.

Tim placed his hands on the wall. There was really nothing for him to grab hold of, but he tried anyway.

It worked!

Tim was suddenly climbing up the wall like Spiderman! He started laughing as he went up and down the wall, back and forth, sideways and upside down!

"WOW!" Tim exclaimed. "It's . . . it's like my hands stick right to the wall! I don't even have to hold on very tight!"

"Now try the ceiling," the Great Tuttworth said, smiling.

Tim climbed up to the ceiling and sure enough, he was able to climb along the flat surface, completely upside down!

"This is GREAT!" he laughed. I laughed too.

Tim leapt from the ceiling and landed on his feet on the floor.

"Cool!" he said.

"And now," the Great Tuttworth said to me. "Try yours."

I was nervous. *Really* nervous.

I mean, I've never flown before, and I'm pretty sure you haven't either. Once I flew on a plane. But I was in a seat and there were a bunch of other people on board.

"How does it work?" I asked. "Do I flap my arms?"

The Great Tuttworth exploded in a fit of laughter. "Of course not!" he said, trying to contain himself.

I didn't know what was so funny. I mean . . . I've never used a stone to fly before.

"Just concentrate on being weightless, on being up in the air," he said.

And so I did.

Imagine my surprise when all of a sudden I found myself off the ground! Tim clapped his hands.

"That's REALLY cool!" he said.

I was able to float around the room, almost like I was swimming in the air! I touched the ceiling, the walls, then flew to the other side of the room and then back to the floor again. It was great!

"But," the old man warned, "you must be careful. You will only be able to fly for a few moments at a time, then you will not be able to use it again for another day. It takes a lot of energy to fly. The poor little stone is not capable of holding any more power. It must rest and recharge before it is used again. But it may prove to be very useful if you find yourself in danger."

I was about to ask him something but suddenly the Great Tuttworth's eyes grew wide.

"Goodness!" he cried. "You must be on your way! Right now! This very minute!" He seemed panicked as he sprang for the door. He unlatched the bolt, quickly opened the door and peered outside. He stared out for a few moments.

"All clear," he said finally.

"What's the matter?" I asked. "Why do we have to leave all of a sudden?"

"It's getting dark. Anyone who remains in the Captive Forest after nightfall becomes a prisoner. But there's still time. You must leave immediately."

The Great Tuttworth began to walk along a stone path that wound along a small creek. The water in the creek was clear and sparkly as it jutted around corners and over rocks. The Miracle-Maker walked quickly, and Tim and I followed him.

Finally he stopped at a spot next to the creek. "Here," he said. "This is where you can get out safely."

"Where?" Tim asked. I was curious, too. I didn't know what the man meant.

"In the water. There's a passageway in the water. When you jump in the currents will pull you deep, but don't be afraid. You'll come up quickly and when you do, you'll be on the other side of the island."

Huh? The other side of the island?

"Why can't we just walk over—" Tim's voice was interrupted by a shrill cry from the sky. I didn't have to look to know what was coming.

Wartwings!

"Hurry!" the Great Tuttworth shouted. "There is no time now! Into the water! Both of you!"

"But where do we find the Stone Key?!?!?" I stammered. "Where is this 'Skull Mountain'?"

"You will find it easily enough," the Great Tuttworth replied quickly. "Now . . . you both must go! Hurry!"

Before I could even speak he grabbed Tim and threw him in the creek! Tim quickly disappeared, swallowed up by the churning waters.

Then the Great Tuttworth grabbed me.

I was next!

He picked me up in the air and threw me into the water.

"Oh!" he shouted to me as I splashed into the creek. "I almost forgot! Watch out for the Blinkmongers!"

Blinkmongers!?!?!?!?

But I didn't have time to ask him anything more. I was being pulled under the water!

13

I felt myself being pulled down into the water. I held my breath, preparing for the worst, when I suddenly splashed to the surface. I had only been under water for a few seconds!

Surprised, I sputtered, exhaled, then drew in a deep breath and looked around. I was in a totally different place!

Tim was already on the surface, and he was treading water just a few feet away. His wet hair clung to his head. My hair had fallen over my face and I reached up to pull it away from my eyes.

We were now in a lake . . . it looked like it could have been Lake Huron. But we were about a hundred feet from shore!

I tried to touch bottom, but it was too deep.

When I looked down, I was amazed to see that I could actually see bottom! It was a long, long ways beneath me. It's a good thing that both Tim and I are good swimmers.

"Come on," I said, and started to crawl toward the shore. Tim did the same.

After several minutes of swimming we reached a rocky shoreline. There were a lot of big boulders and stones. Some were as big as cars. Even bigger. Beyond the shore I could see towering pines and maple trees. It looked like it could actually be Mackinac Island. For a minute I thought that we *were* on Mackinac Island!

That is, until I saw a movement behind some trees.

"Tim!" I whispered frantically. "Look!"

I pointed in the direction of where I had seen the motion.

Whatever it was, it was looking the other way. I couldn't see it real well. And it hadn't seen us.

Yet.

"Let's hide," I whispered.

Tim followed me over to a big rock. He peaked around one edge and I peaked around the other.

I could see more movement from behind the trees, and then the creature was in full view.

When I saw it I realized that I was *definitely* not on Mackinac Island.

It looked kind of like a monkey. A big monkey with long arms. It was covered with dark brown hair.

But when it turned, I could see two huge eyes! Each eye was almost the size of its head! It kept blinking its eyes, faster and faster, and—

Ah-ha!

That's what the Great Tuttworth had tried to warn us about! Blinkmongers!

But what were they?

I guess it was kind of scary looking. It was bigger than me and Tim.

I'm glad we saw it before it saw us!

Suddenly there was a loud noise, like two sticks being hit together.

And someone was shouting!

"Git! Go'wan, GIT!" The Blinkmonger took off running and soon disappeared into the forest.

I don't know what I was expecting to see, but I sure wasn't prepared for what came next.

Because sharp claws suddenly dug into my shoulders and I was jerked off the ground and into the air! Suddenly I was sailing upward, looking at the ground below me, quickly speeding farther and farther away.

Oh no! I had been captured by a Wartwing!

14

I could see Tim below, still standing by the rock. His figure was getting smaller and smaller as the creature carried me higher into the air.

I was way above the treetops, but I couldn't do anything! The Wartwing's claws dug into my shoulder. There was nothing I could do.

This was definitely NOT a good thing.

Just then something whizzed by my head. I couldn't see what it was, but I could tell the direction it came from. Another object suddenly hurled up from the ground.

In a small clearing stood someone . . . a man, it looked like. He had a slingshot. He was shooting at me!

One of the objects struck the Wartwing and

the creature let out a yell.

Then I figured it out. The man on the ground wasn't shooting at me . . . *he was aiming for the Wartwing!*

The next object hit the creature square in the nose. It screeched an awful, ear-piercing wail—

And let me go! Suddenly I was falling through the air!

I'm a goner!

The wind whirled past and I could hear my brother shouting something as I plummeted towards the ground.

What was he saying?

Then I could hear him.

"FLY!" he was shouting. *"FLY! JUST LIKE THE GREAT TUTTWORTH SHOWED YOU!"*

Let me tell you, if I ever needed that silly rock to work, it was NOW!

I concentrated hard and felt my body slowing.

It was working! It was really working! I began to fall slower and slower and slower. I could feel myself gaining control, gently lowering myself to the ground.

And not a moment too soon, either. By the time I gained full control of the fall I was almost on the ground.

Boy . . . I sure was glad I had that stone.

Tim came running up to me.

"I thought you were gone for sure!" he said.

I thought he was going to hug me, but he didn't.

"Me too," I replied shakily. "I thought that thing had me for good."

"Why did he let you go?" Tim asked.

I was about to tell him about the man with the slingshot when I heard more movement by the trees. We were still standing by the water's edge when a man suddenly appeared.

Actually, I thought it was a man at first . . . but when he got closer, I could see that he was far too small. He was short and squat, with a beanie-type hat.

It was a gnome!

I mean a real life, honest-to-goodness gnome, just like you'd expect a gnome to look like. He was wearing red bib overalls and wore a full beard and mustache. He looked like one of Snow White's Seven Dwarfs!

I wasn't sure if we should run or not, but I figured that we weren't in any danger. Besides . . . he had just saved my life.

"You two had better be more careful," he said, approaching us. "Wartwings are nasty, nasty things."

"Thank you for scaring him off," I said.

"All in a day's work," he replied.

He stopped a few feet in front of us. He was tiny! He was probably no more than two feet tall! I have never seen anyone so small before.

"What are two kids like you doing here on the

Isle of Mayhem?" he asked.

"Well, it wasn't really our choice," I answered. "I'm not sure how we got here, but we have to find the Stone Key before we can get home."

His eyes grew huge, and he looked at me in amazement.

"The Stone Key?!?!" *THE* Stone Key?!?!"

"Yes," I answered. "The Great Tuttworth says that if we find the key, he can go home and so can we."

"No one has ever found the Stone Key," the little man responded.

My heart sank.

"We have to find it," Tim spoke up. "We have to. Or else we'll never get home."

"Well, you can try. There's been a lot of people who have tried. Poor souls."

"Poor souls?" I asked. "What do you mean?"

"They were never heard from again," he said, shaking his head. "No one who's gone looking for the Stone Key has ever returned."

This was NOT looking good.

"But we have to find it," I insisted. We just *have* to. The Great Tuttworth says that it is somewhere inside of Skull Mountain. Do you know how to get there?"

The gnome paused a minute. He looked at us like we were out of our minds! Then he turned and raised his arm. He pointed over the treetops.

"There."

Both Tim and I looked in the direction he was pointing.

Suddenly we saw what he was talking about. I had thought it was just a mountain of rock, but now that I looked closer, I could make it out. What I saw sent chills through my body.

It was a skull.

The biggest skull I had ever seen. It must have been ten stories high. It sat at the top of the mountain. Even from where we were I could see the huge shapes of Wartwings swarming in the sky around it.

"What is THAT?" I asked. But I already knew. I think I just had to ask because I didn't know what else to say.

"Skull Mountain. It's the most terrible, most wretched place on the Isle of Mayhem. That is where the key is. Somewhere inside. Somewhere inside the skull."

Tim and I just stared. How were we going to get up there? Especially with all those Wartwings flying around?

Have you ever taken a test at school and just *knew* that you were going to fail?

That's how I felt right then. Only ten times worse.

Tim and I were staring at Skull Mountain for so long that we didn't even see what was creeping up behind us. The gnome spotted it first.

"Look out!" he cried.

Tim and I turned, alarmed.

In the water, not twenty feet behind us, were the biggest pair of eyes I had ever seen! Eyes the size of garbage can lids. They were just above the surface of the water, moving toward us. I knew instantly what they were. Those eyes belonged to the thing that I think frightens me worst of all.

Those eyes belonged to a snake.

And judging by the size of its eyes, the snake would have to be as big around as a train!

15

A snake.

There was no mistake, especially as it got closer. It was a hideous thing, with giant scales and a long, worm-like tongue. It slithered through the water, coming closer and closer.

"It's one of King Balderdash's giant sea-snakes," the gnome whispered. "Be very still. I don't think he can see you. Its eyesight is very poor, and if you remain still, it won't know you're there."

How can you stay still when a forty-foot long snake is right in front of you?

Actually, it was easier than I thought, because I was frozen. I was so scared I couldn't move.

The snake's head came all the way up out of the water. Its tongue flicked in and out. It looked absolutely dreadful!

Tim started shaking. He's caught some snakes, and he used to scare me with them.

But I don't think he was planning on catching this one!

The snake's long, flickering tongue came within inches from my face. I could see its eyes looking around, darting from side to side. I sure hoped that the gnome was right. I hoped the snake couldn't see us.

The snake's giant head moved back and forth. I think it could sense that something was there, but it wasn't sure what. I tried to stay as still as possible.

I'm not sure how long the three of us stayed there, waiting. It seemed like forever. Finally, the snake slowly sunk back into the water. I watched it dip beneath the surface before I moved or said anything. We waited for a few minutes, unmoving, to make sure the snake had returned to the depths.

"That was close," I finally said, relieved that the snake had passed us by. The gnome spoke.

"Using his dark magic, King Balderdash has filled the waters with his awful sea-snakes," he said. "That way, no one can try to leave. We're all trapped."

Tim was still so scared he couldn't speak.

"But where do you live?" I asked the small man.

"I live underground. Most of us here on the

Isle of Mayhem must live underground or in caves. When we do come out, we have to be very careful."

It didn't sound like living on the Isle of Mayhem was very much fun.

"Can you take us to Skull Mountain?" I asked the gnome.

"It is far away," he replied. "I can take you as far as the River of Dreams, and that's where I stop. But I can help you get that far."

"River of Dreams?" Tim asked. It was the first words he had spoken since the snake had left.

"That's a river you must cross. Gnomes can't cross it, or else we'd become lost in Dreamland for sure."

"Dreamland?" I asked. This place was getting stranger by the minute.

"You don't want to go there," the gnome replied. That's where all dreams—good and bad—come from. If you fall into the River of Dreams, you'd better watch out. Nothing is real anymore until you get out. *If* you get out. Most people . . . gnomes included . . . never find their way out of the River of Dreams."

The gnome stopped talking and he looked at us. I could tell that he was very concerned. "Are you sure you still want to go?" he asked.

"I'm afraid we have to," I replied.

"Yeah," Tim answered. He didn't sound very enthused. "The sooner we find that dumb key, the sooner we can get back to the real Mackinac Island."

I took another look above the treetops and caught another glimpse of Skull Mountain. There were dark clouds around it now and I could see bright flashes of lightning. A few Wartwings were circling around the clouds. It looked very scary.

All of a sudden I knew where I was!

"Tim!" I exclaimed. "We're on Mackinac Island right now!"

He looked at me like I was from Mars, and he drew his eyebrows together.

"What are you talking about?" he said.

I pointed my finger in the air. "Look at where the mountain is! Look at the hills! Look at where we're standing! We're on Mackinac Island, only this is some sort of other dimension or something! We're standing right where the marina should be!"

I couldn't believe it, but for once in his life, Tim agreed with me.

"You're right!" he said suddenly, looking around. "Over there would be the center of town—" he pointed, then continued. "—and over there is where the Grand Hotel should be!"

"What is this 'Mackinac Island' you're talking about?" the tiny gnome asked.

"It's where we live," I answered. "It's our home. At least, during the summer it is."

"And the Stone Key will help you get back there?" he asked.

"That's what the Great Tuttworth says," Tim replied.

"Well, then, let's see what we can do about getting you home."

And with that the gnome started off, and Tim and I followed. We were off to Skull Mountain.

But first we had to cross the River of Dreams.

I thought that it should be easy. I thought that all we would have to do is cross on some bridge or maybe rocks that stuck out of the water. I thought all we would have to do is cross without falling in.

You can't imagine how wrong a girl can be. I had no idea of the danger that we were about to face.

16

The River of Dreams was appropriately named. It was beautiful! Colorful flowers grew all along the river banks, and the water was just as cool and blue as I'd ever seen. It looked so refreshing and clean, but the gnome changed my ideas about that.

"Poison," he said. "The River of Dreams is the deadliest poison on the Isle of Mayhem. One drop is all it takes. If you get so much as a single drop on your skin, you're in Dreamland. You'll have to be very careful."

"How are we going to cross?" I asked. I didn't see a bridge or anything. And there were no stones to walk on.

"There's a fallen tree down around the next bend," the gnome replied. "You can walk across there."

I reached into my pocket and felt for my stone. It was still there, but I remembered what the Great Tuttworth had told me.

I could only use the stone to fly once a day. I had already used it once today. That meant I couldn't fly to the other side of the river.

How much easier it would have been if I could have just flown to the other side!

We walked for a few more minutes until we came to the tree that had fallen. It was like any tree you'd expect to see, almost like the pine trees that grow on Mackinac Island. Except the bark was a deep, golden brown. It looked like it had been dead for a long time.

"You'll need to walk across the tree trunk to get to the other side," the gnome said, standing a few feet from the river. "But whatever you do, don't look into the water when you cross it! That's the most dangerous part."

Both Tim and I looked at the gnome. He must have seen the puzzled expressions on our faces, because he continued.

"If you look into the water, you'll become instantly hypnotized by your very own dreams. It's very powerful. You will feel that if you just jumped into the water, all of your dreams will come true. That's how many people come to fall into the River of Dreams."

"What would happen then?" Tim asked.

"If you went into the water," the gnome answered, "everything becomes an illusion. You become lost in a world of your own imagination."

"Cool! I'll imagine a million dollars!" Tim said.

That's my brother for you.

"The trouble with that," the gnome answered, "is that your worst nightmares also come true."

Tim and I were both silent. I certainly didn't want my nightmares coming true! What was happening right now on the Isle of Mayhem was bad enough.

"Hey!" Tim said, his eyes growing wide. "This will be easy! I can climb just like a spider!" He pulled out the stone in his pocket. "And you can just climb on my back, Sandy! I'll just stare at the tree so I won't look at the water! You can close your eyes. It'll work!"

I had to admit it was a good idea. I hate it when my brother has a good idea.

"Let's give it a try," I said.

Tim got on his hands and knees and climbed on the edge of the tree that lay long-ways over the river. "Come on, Sandy," he said.

"Okay," I said. "But you'd better go slow."

And so we started off, slowly, across the river.

Tim was able to climb along with his hands and feet very easily. He was sure footed and secure, just like a spider would be.

"Remember what I told you about looking into the water!" the gnome shouted to us.

"Okay!" I shouted back. "And thank you for your help!"

"Don't mention it! Oh . . . and don't forget! Watch out for the Blinkmongers!"

"The *what!?!?*" I shouted back.

But the gnome had disappeared.

Suddenly we stopped.

"Tim, what's wrong?" I asked.

No answer.

"Tim?" I asked again, already fearing the worst.

"Tim, knock it off. Keep going."

But he still didn't answer me.

When I looked into his eyes, my fears were confirmed.

Tim had opened his eyes. He had become hypnotized by the River of Dreams.

17

"Tim!" I shouted. "Tim! You're hypnotized! Wake up! WAKE UP!"

But it was no use. He ignored me just like he ignores me on Saturday mornings when he's watching TV.

Now remember: all of this is happening and I can't look at the river. If I did, then I'd be hypnotized just like Tim.

Then we'd *never* get home.

I had no idea what to do. The gnome was gone, and I was stranded. Tim was frozen. We were stuck on a tree in the middle of the river.

But I remembered what the gnome had said. Tim was only hypnotized. He hadn't touched any water.

Not yet, anyway.

Maybe there was still a chance.

I had to find a way to break him out of his trance.

I figured the first thing I would need to do was to get him to stop looking at the river, so I put my hand over his eyes.

"Tim!" I hollered again. "TIM!!"

Still no luck.

"At the count of three you're going to wake up!" I commanded. "One . . ."

Tim remained still, frozen to the fallen tree.

"Two . . . ."

Still nothing.

"Three!"

Nope. It was becoming more hopeless by the minute. I couldn't just leave him there!

Okay. I had one last idea. It was drastic, and I didn't want to do it, but it was the only thing left to do. I leaned forward and whispered into his ear.

"Tim, if you don't wake up this instant, I'm throwing all of your comic books away. And all of your video games."

It was like a lightning bolt struck him! His eyes opened and he turned his head, facing me.

"If you do," he said, "I'll put glue in your hair when you're sleeping!"

He was back.

"Don't look at the water again!" I warned

him, and I covered his eyes with my hands. He looked confused, like he didn't know where he was or what was going on. I told him what happened.

"You were hypnotized by the River of Dreams," I said. "Now . . . be careful. Don't look at the water again." I pulled my hands away from his face.

He crept forward slowly. I held on around his neck, making sure that he looked at the tree and not at the churning waters below.

After what seemed like hours (it was really only about a minute) we made it to the other side. I looked back over the water, and I was shocked by what I saw.

All of the flowers were dead!

The water was a dirty brown, and it indeed looked like poison like the gnome had said. It didn't look at all like the river from the other side! I guess that's what the gnome was trying to tell us about both dreams and nightmares. On one side of the river we saw the dreamy part, and on this side, the nightmares.

What a weird, weird world this was.

"That was close," Tim said.

"You're not kidding," I replied. "Come on. We have to get up to Skull Mountain and find that key."

The going was really tough. There were lots of rocks and trees and no path. I stumbled a couple times. Tim fell once and skinned his knee through his denim jeans.

But we had a bigger problem then that. It was getting dark.

And as it got darker, the shadows grew longer. Everything looked really spooky.

"S . . . s . . . s . . . Sandy?" Tim stuttered.

"What?" I answered.

Tim stopped. He was pointing at something.

I looked, and now I wish I hadn't. I wish he would have just told me what he saw.

Because when I looked, I could see dozens of pairs of glowing red eyes, staring at us from the shadows, hiding behind branches and bushes.

18

Do you know what those eyes looked like?

Fireflies. They looked like little red fireflies, blinking and flashing in the darkness.

But I knew they weren't. I knew that they were eyes, and that they were watching us.

I was terrified!

In the dark I couldn't tell how far away they were. I couldn't even tell what kind of creature they belonged to.

But I was about to find out.

One of the pairs of eyes were coming toward us!

Tim and I froze. I felt like running, but where would we run to?

The creature stopped a few feet away.

It was a dog! It was medium-sized, about waist-high. It looked just like any ordinary dog.

Except for one BIG detail.

What was REALLY strange . . . and even quite frightening . . . was that the dog had two horns protruding from each side of its head!

"Ahem," the dog began in a squeaky, high-pitched voice. "And whom do I have the pleasure of addressing?"

"Huh?" Tim said.

Typical brother.

"My name is Sandy," I spoke up. "And this is my brother Tim. We don't want to hurt anyone. And we hope you don't want to hurt us." My voice was trembling as I spoke.

"Hurt you?" the voice peeped. "Oh nonsense, nonsense."

Suddenly I heard voices echoing from the darkness. "Nonsense! Nonsense!" they said.

"What . . . what are you?" Tim asked.

"My name is Bartholomew. You may call me Bart. And I am a bulldog. Anyone can see that."

I laughed, because it just seemed a bit funny. A dog with horns?!?! I get it! A BULLdog! It really seemed quite funny.

"I beg your pardon, Miss," the dog said. He sounded a bit upset. "But what do you find so funny?"

"I'm sorry," I said. "It's just that I've never

seen a dog with horns before."

"Well, what would you expect a bulldog to have? Wings?"

"Well, I guess not," I replied. I kept staring at the dog and his two horns. "I'm sorry. I didn't mean to make fun of you."

"Apology accepted. But what are *you* two doing on the Isle of Mayhem? It's almost dark, you know. No one comes out after dark on the Isle of Mayhem."

"We've got to go to Skull Mountian," Tim interjected.

Hearing this, the other bulldogs still hidden in the shadows began to howl.

"Skull Mountain?!?!?" Bart barked. "Why on *earth* do you want to go to Skull Mountain?!?!"

"To get the Stone Key," I said. "We can't go home until we find the Stone Key."

At this, the dogs let out another howl. It was eerie. All that wailing reminded me of howling wolves.

"Well, certainly you don't plan to go to Skull Mountain at night?" Bart the bulldog said.

"Well, we—"

"I mean . . . no one comes out at night on the Isle of Mayhem. Too many Wartwings, those awful creatures. And Blinkmongers."

There was that name again. Blinkmonger.

"What's a Blinkmonger?" I asked.

"Well, you might find out right now," the bulldog said. "There's two of them behind you."

19

Tim and I both turned and sure enough, two huge dark forms were approaching.

"What do we do?" I whispered.

"At this point," the bulldog said matter-of-factly, "it would probably be in your best interest to run."

I was REALLY beginning to not like this place.

"Follow me!" Bart suddenly barked, spinning on his paws.

The other dogs let out howls and yips and Tim and I followed the bulldog as he bounded through the forest.

By now it had grown very dark and the going was tough. It was hard to see the ground, and both

Tim and I stumbled all over the place.

"Keep running," the bulldog ordered. He was running just a few feet in front of us. "Blinkmongers are slow. And they're not very smart, either. We can outrun them."

"But what's so bad about them?" I stuttered while trying to run.

"I'll tell you later. Ah! Here we are!"

All of a sudden most of the dogs were gone and I saw the bulldog disappear too. Tim and I stopped, bewildered. We were at the foot of the mountain, and before us was nothing but a wall of solid rock.

"Where are you?" I cried. I could hear the Blinkmonger thundering through the forest not far behind. In a minute he would be upon us!

"Over here!" I heard Bart the bulldog yip. Tim and I followed the sound of his voice and we came to a small cave. The opening wasn't very big. Tim and I both had to bend down on our hands and knees to get through.

We crawled for what seemed like a long time, and then the small tunnel opened up into a large cavern! There were lights and furniture and tables. It looked like a home for people and not one for a dog!

"Do you like my humble domicile?" Bart asked.

"Yes, it's nice," I replied, not sure what a

'domicile' was, but pretty sure he was talking about his home.

"You may stay here tonight if you wish," the dog offered. "I don't think you'll want to be out there when Blinkmongers are around."

"That's very kind of you," I said. I was going to ask him about the Blinkmongers but I began to feel very tired. Tim did too, and I could see his eyes getting heavy.

"I'm getting very . . . ."

That was the last thing I remembered.

The next thing I knew I woke up on the couch. Tim was sleeping beside me.

But Bart was nowhere to be found!

20

"Hello?" I said, hoping the dog was around somewhere. My voice woke Tim up and he rubbed his eyes.

Boy . . . were Mom and Dad going to be mad at us! We'd been gone overnight. They probably had everyone looking for us.

I was sure that we would be grounded for the rest of our lives when we got home.

That is, *if* we got home. I was beginning to have my doubts.

"Where do you suppose the dog went?" Tim asked.

"I don't know," I said. I stood up and stretched. "But we can't wait to find out. We have to find the Stone Key and get back home."

We climbed down on our hands and knees and crawled out the tunnel where we came in. After a few minutes we were outside again, standing in the sunshine.

Still no bulldogs! Bart had disappeared.

I looked high up into the air, and so did Tim. In the distance, we could see the giant skull at the top of the mountain. It looked so cold and dreadful. And SCARY. Scarier than ever.

That was the LAST place I wanted to go!

But we had to.

"How are we going to get up there?" I asked.

"Easy," Tim said. "You can fly and I can crawl. We have our stones. Remember?"

"No, I don't want to fly. Remember what the Great Tuttworth said? I can only fly once a day. I don't want to fly unless I absolutely have to."

After walking around at the bottom of the mountain for a few minutes, we came to a steep path that led up the mountain. It was almost like steps carved in stone.

"Cool," Tim said. "This will be easy."

And he was right. Walking up the side and around the mountain was like walking up stairs. It was tiring, but it was easier than rock climbing like I've seen those guys on TV.

But then I began to notice something. The farther to the top we got, the darker it became. Storm clouds appeared, and I could see bolts of lightning flashing within them.

But below us in the valley was bright sunshine! It seemed the only place that was shrouded in dark clouds was Skull Mountain.

It was spooky.

But not as spooky as what I saw when I looked back up . . . .

21

When I looked up, I could see that we were right at the bottom of the giant skull. It towered above us!

Tim looked up. "Wow," he said quietly. I think he was a little scared, too.

"Let's keep going," I said. But when we took a few more steps forward, the stone stairs suddenly stopped.

"What in the world!?!?!?" Tim said. "Who would make steps that end right at a solid wall of rock?"

I had to agree with him. It sure was odd.

I looked around for the path to continue somewhere else.

But it didn't! The steps led right up to a wall of solid rock, then stopped.

Suddenly the clouds opened up and it began to rain. The wind began to howl.

"We have to do something!" I yelled over the coming storm. The wind blew my hair all around and the rain beat at my face. Both Tim and I were quickly soaked to the skin.

Suddenly, Tim became very angry.

"I don't like this place! I don't like this place at all!" he yelled. "I don't like Wartwings and I don't like Blinkmongers and giant snakes and the River of Dreams! I want to go home!"

In his frustration he reached out and slapped the rock wall in front of him.

A door opened!

It was a secret door that the steps led to! The rock wall rolled away before us and the steps continued inside the giant skull.

Tim stood back in amazement. I just looked into the tunnel, amazed. A stone stairway led up into the giant skull. There were lit torches along the wall.

"It sure looks scary," Tim said.

THAT was the understatement of the year.

"Come on," I said. "We have to keep going."

Tim, all of a sudden, wasn't so sure.

"I'm not going in there," he said. "It's too spooky."

By now the wind was really blowing and the rain was coming down even harder.

"We don't have a choice, Tim," I said,

pushing him forward. Just as I did, a lightning bolt ripped out of the sky and struck right where Tim had been standing! It was so close our hair stood on end!

I leaped into the tunnel and stood next to Tim.

"Gosh Sandy . . . thanks. Thanks a lot. I almost got cooked back there."

I was going to tell him that he was welcome when the rock wall suddenly slid closed behind us!

We were trapped. Now there was no way to go but up.

Up into Skull Mountain.

22

Our footsteps echoed through the corridor as we began the steep climb up the stone staircase. The lanterns lit our way, but it still was scary.

I felt like I was in one of those old, old castles. Like Dracula's castle! I kept expecting to see a vampire leap out from a hidden doorway. None did, and I was glad.

The steps wound up and around and seemed to go on forever. I was tired, and so was Tim.

Just when I didn't think I could go any farther, the steps stopped and we came to a large room. The ceiling was very high and the room was huge. But we couldn't go in because of an iron gate! Actually, we could easily jump over the gate, but it was there to keep people out. It was just a steel rail that went across the tunnel. And there was a sign on the wall that read:

STOP! NO ADMITTANCE WITHOUT TICKETS!

"Huh?" Tim said. "What's that supposed to mean?"

I didn't know what the sign meant, and I was tired from the long climb. "Let's rest a minute," I said.

Suddenly we were shaken by a loud voice that was very close to us!

"TICKETS!" the voice boomed.

I jumped and spun on my heels and so did Tim. The voice was so loud and close it had scared the daylights out of me.

Right before us in the wall was a window! Not a glass window, but just an opening in the wall. There were steel bars going across it.

It looked like a ticket window, just like at the skating rink.

There was a man in a blue uniform sitting at the counter on the other side of the window. He had a blue cap and a thick mustache.

"TICKETS!" he boomed again. "I need your tickets, please."

"Tickets?!?!" I stammered. "We . . . we don't have any tickets."

"NO TICKETS? NO ADMITTANCE!" He looked angry and he pointed at the sign.

And with that he pulled down a dark shade that covered the window. A sign came down with the shade.

The sign read 'CLOSED.'

"Now what?" Tim asked.

"Maybe if we buy some tickets, he'll let us go through," I said.

I leaned forward, my face nearing the bars.

"Uh, excuse, me, sir," I said very meekly. "But we'd like to buy some tickets."

The shade snapped up!

"Well then, well then," the man said, smiling and folding his hands. "What'll that be? Balcony? Front row . . . we have—"

"What are the tickets for?" Tim asked.

The man looked at Tim curiously. "Why, they're for the show," he replied.

"What show?" I asked.

"The Stone Key show," the man responded. "Would you like to see it? We have some good seats left."

"What on earth is the 'Stone Key' show?" Tim asked. I wanted to know too!

"Come now!" the man said. "Everyone has heard of the Stone Key show. It's about a couple of kids who try and steal the Stone Key from Skull Mountain. They have all kinds of problems, then they wind up getting eaten by Blinkmongers."

Oh no!

"That's horrible!" I gasped.

"Actually," the man said, "It's quite good. Quite good indeed. Now . . . did you want balcony or floor seats?"

Tim suddenly spoke up. "Give us two floor seats, please," he said.

I stared at him. What was he doing?!?!? We didn't have any money!

But Tim just smiled.

"Two floor seats it is," the man said. He turned around for a moment and Tim grabbed me by the arm.

"Now!" he whispered, and suddenly he jumped over the metal gate! Now I understood what he had done. Tim had distracted the ticket man just long enough to give us time to slip away!

I leapt over the gate after Tim. He was already running through the large cavern, heading towards a tunnel on the other side. I followed him into the darkened passageway, and I could hear the ticket man shouting behind us.

"Guards! Guards! SEIZE THEM! SEIZE THEM!"

I could tell that whatever was about to happen, it was not going to be good.

Alarms began to sound. I could hear men shouting. They were coming after us!

But I didn't have to worry. The guards weren't going to be our big problem.

Our big problem came as we ran down the dark cave. It was hard to see but we pressed onward, running as fast as we could.

To where, I could only guess. We kept running down the tunnel, around corners and down narrow passageways.

Tim was still in front of me when suddenly he let out a scream and disappeared!

Before I knew what was wrong, I was screaming, too. Not just because I was scared.

But because I was now falling, tumbling through the darkness in a free fall!

23

Splash!

Below me, I heard the sound of Tim plunging into water. Suddenly I hit the water with a heavy *ker-splash!* It was dark and I was underwater, but then my head popped above the surface.

"Tim!" I shouted. "Tim?!?!?"

"I'm here!" he said. Thankfully, he was close by.

Once again, I was never so glad to hear his voice. We had fallen into some sort of underground pool. Oh, how I wish we were back on Mackinac Island!

"Are you okay?" I asked.

"Yeah," Tim sputtered. "But I can't see you."

"Me neither," I said. "It's too dark."

"By the way our voices are echoing, we must be in some well of some sort."

I heard splashing water.

"Just as I thought," Tim said, his voice a few feet farther away. "It's a wall."

I could hear him swim around the perimeter of the pool. "See?" he said. "It's not very big."

"Is there anything to grab hold of?" I asked.

"No," he replied. "I think that if there was ever a time to use our stones, it's now."

I didn't really want to, but this really *was* an emergency. How else would we be able to get out?

"I'll go first," he said. "That way, I can climb up to make sure that no one has chased us in here. If it's all clear I'll come back to get you."

"Be careful," I said.

"Don't worry, Munchkin," he said.

For the first time in my life I didn't mind being called Munchkin.

Tim swam to the side of the cavern. I heard lots of water swishing.

And more.

"What's wrong?" I asked.

"I . . . I don't know," Tim said. "I . . . I can't seem to climb. It doesn't seem—"

I could hear him struggling, trying to climb the wall. "It doesn't seem to work! I can't climb up!"

Then he said what I had already begun to

think.

"Sandy! I can't find my stone! It's not in my pocket!"

Beneath the water I dug my hand into the pocket of my jeans.

My stone was gone too!

We had fallen deep into a cavern filled with water. I thought maybe we lost the stones in the fall.

However we had lost them didn't matter at the time. What mattered was that we were a long ways from home, stuck in a dark well somewhere deep within Skull Mountain.

Tim and I were about as trapped as two people could be.

We felt all alone.

But we were about to realize that we weren't the only ones swimming around in the dark water.

24

Tim noticed it first.

"S . . . S . . . Sandy?" he said quietly. His voice was tense and I immediately knew that something was wrong.

I didn't have to ask, because he spoke again.

"S . . . s . . . something just touched my leg."

We both froze. All we could hear was the lapping of the water against the side of the slippery stone.

Suddenly something brushed my leg under water!

"I just felt it, too," I said, my voice trembling.

Now I was *really* scared.

Just then the water in front of us exploded! Both Tim and I screamed. Our eyes were becoming adjusted to the dark and we could make out the form of someone . . . or *something* . . . in the water in front of us. Tim and I stayed quiet now, both of us too afraid to speak.

"Well, hey there, hi there, ho there," a deep voice finally said.

I must say that although I was still very scared, the voice sounded friendly, and I managed to speak.

"Who . . . who are you?" I asked.

"My name is Warren Otterpuss, at your service. The only Otterpuss on the Isle of Mayhem."

"The only *what?*" Tim squeaked.

"Why, an Otterpuss, of course!" the deep voice boomed, echoing up the cavern walls.

An Otterpuss? I had never heard of such a thing. Of course, I was quickly learning that there were a lot of things on the Isle of Mayhem that I hadn't heard about. Like dogs with horns that were called Bulldogs. And those really ugly Wartwings and Blinkmongers. Whatever *they* were.

"What's an Otterpuss?" I asked.

"Oh, please, oh please," the voice said proudly. "Allow me, allow me. An Otterpuss is one of those rare creatures that is a cross between an Otter and an Octopus. Handy, friendly, helpful, and always, always very polite and willing to lend a hand. Eight of them, actually. You happen to be conversing with an Otterpuss at this very moment."

"That's . . . uh . . . that's nice," I said finally, not knowing what else to say.

"The pleasure is all mine, all mine, to be sure, to be sure," the Otterpuss said. He really was very friendly.

"Will you help us?" Tim asked. "We're kind of in a jam."

"Ah yes," the Otterpuss chuckled. "A jam, a fix, a quandary, a problem. A complication, an annoyance, a complexity, a concern. Tell me. What kind of conundrum do you find yourself in?"

"Uh . . . I beg your pardon?" I asked.

"Conundrum. You know. A jam, a fix, a quandary, a problem. A complication, and annoyance, a complexity, a—"

"We're stuck here," Tim interrupted. "We fell into this well or whatever it is and now we can't get out."

"Ah yes. Say no more. If out is what you want, out is what you'll get. Warren Otterpuss is at your service, thank you very much. Very much indeed. That's what Otterpusses do best you know. Lend a hand, as many as needed, up to eight if necessary. Now . . . take a deep breath please."

What? A deep breath? What was going on?

Nevertheless, I had just taken a deep breath, not knowing what was going to happen when a thick, rubbery arm wrapped around me! Squishy tentacles gripped me tight. I was being pulled underwater!

25

Beneath the surface it was very dark. I could feel water rushing by as I was pulled deeper and deeper.

What's going on? I thought. *Where's Tim?*

It was impossible to see in the dark depths. I knew I was being dragged deeper beneath the surface, but I didn't know where I was going. I couldn't see anything.

THAT is a very scary feeling!

Another thing that scared me was being under water for a long time. I could already feel my lungs start to hurt from being under water for so long. It seemed like an hour had gone by, but actually it was less than a minute.

But *wait* . . . .

Suddenly the water became less murky and

dark.

I could see light! It was faint, but we were rushing towards it. It was the surface!

I could see the strange arms that were now pulling me up. Tim was not far away. He, too, was being held tightly by the Otterpuss.

And then we were on the surface, the water splashing all around us. The sun was shining, the sky was blue and a few puffy white clouds drifted across the sky. I took a deep, thankful breath, and both Tim and I swam to shore a few feet away. Warren Otterpuss stayed in the water.

Now, about Warren Otterpuss.

In the dark cave, I could only see his form. Now in the bright daylight I could see him for the first time—and what a sight he was!

Warren Otterpuss looked exactly like he said he was—a cross between an otter and an octopus! I must say I've never seen anything like him. He had eight arms like an octopus, but his body wasn't all slimy and rubbery. It was covered with a layer of thin, fine fur that gleamed in the sunshine. He had the nose of an otter with long, dark whiskers, and two big blue eyes and small, pointy ears.

He actually looked cute! Strange, yes . . . but he didn't look like he would hurt a flea. I was glad for that!

"There we are, there we are," he said, bobbing at the surface. "All safe and sound, all safe and sound."

"Thank you," I said.

"Not a mention, not a mention," Warren Otterpuss replied. I began to think that he repeated everything twice.

"I'm almost afraid to ask," Tim began, looking around. "But . . . where are we?"

"Why, you're on the Isle of Mayhem, the Isle of Mayhem," the Otterpuss answered.

"Yes . . . but where?" I asked.

"You are in my private pond in the Valley of the Bones, yes indeed."

"Valley of the Bones?!?!" I exclaimed. "But we were just in Skull Mountain!"

"True, True," Warren Otterpuss explained. "The Valley of the Bones is just beneath Skull Mountain. You may thank me for pulling you out of Skull Mountain and leading you to safety."

"Well, thank you, Mr. Otterpuss," I offered. "But we need to go back into the Mountian."

At this, Warren Otterpuss scrunched his nose together, flaring his whiskers. His ears flickered back and forth. "Why on earth would you want to go back into Skull Mountain?" he asked. He truly was bewildered.

"We have to find the Stone Key," Tim chimed in.

Hearing this, Warren Otterpuss's eyes grew wide. He shook his head from side to side, ducked beneath the surface of the water, then popped his head out.

"There," he said reassuringly. "That's better. I must be hearing things."

He laughed, a deep, funny laugh that echoed over the small pond. "For a moment there, I thought you said you were looking for the Stone Key."

"We are," I said. "We have to find the Stone Key so we can go home to Mackinac Island."

"The Stone *KEY?!?* Oh dear. Yes, oh dear indeed. The Stone Key. No one's ever found the Stone Key."

"Well, we have to," Tim said. "It's the only way we can go home."

"Oh my. Oh dear. Oh my and oh dear."

It was easy to see that Warren Otterpuss was very distraught by the news that we wanted to return to Skull Mountain.

"Will you help us?" I asked. "Please? We just have to find that key, or we'll be stuck here for good."

Warren Otterpuss looked at me, and then at Tim.

"Well, I—"

All of a sudden he was interrupted by a loud shriek from the sky. A dark shadow swept over the pond. All three of us looked up, terrified.

Wartwings!

26

There were three of them this time. We looked up and they were dropping out of the sky, coming right toward us! The Wartwings screeched again as they sped down, gaining speed and momentum with every passing moment.

"Quick! Back into the pond!" Warren Otterpuss said.

He didn't have to tell us twice!

We dove headfirst into the pond just as the Wartwings screeched down. I could almost feel their sharp claws digging into my shoulders, pulling up and away, carrying me into the air.

I was relieved when I hit the water. I kept diving downward, pushing myself away from the surface. If we'd waited one more second we would've been goners!

Suddenly I felt the strong arms of Warren Otterpuss around me. He was pulling me again!

This time, he pulled us through an underwater cave, and we popped up in a pool of water inside a big room. The pool wasn't very big . . . maybe about as big around as a wading pool. There were no windows in the room. The walls were rough and made of stone, and there was a small table and chair next to the water's edge. I wondered why Warren Otterpuss would need a table and chair if he never left the water.

"Welcome to my home," Warren Otterpuss said. "You're safe now. Those nasty Wartwings can't get us here."

"You live here?" Tim asked.

"Quite so, quite so," the creature replied. "It's most comfortable, most comfortable. You may stay here if you like. I have a table and chairs for guests. Of course, I don't get many guests on the Isle of Mayhem." He motioned toward the furniture with one of his long, tentacle-like arms.

"Well, thank you very much, Mr. Otterpuss," I said. "But we really have to find that key so we can go home. Our mom and dad are probably looking for us right now."

"Oh yes, Oh yes, the Stone Key," Otterpuss pondered. "Somewhere buried deep within Skull Mountain."

"Do you know where it is?" Tim asked.

"Oh no, oh no," Otterpuss said, shaking his head and drawing his long whiskers together. "No one knows exactly where the Stone Key is. It's been lost for thousands of years, thousands of years. Oh, how I wish I knew where it is."

"But it *is* in Skull Mountain somewhere, isn't it?" I asked.

"Yes indeed, yes indeed," Otterpuss answered, bobbing his head. "It's there somewhere. And if you must find it—" he stopped in mid-sentence, and he looked at Tim, then at me. "—if you *must* find it, then I can show you a secret way in. It's a tunnel that no one knows about except myself," he finished proudly.

"But how will we know where to look?" Tim asked.

That was a good question. Unfortunately, Warren Otterpuss didn't have the answer I was hoping for.

"No idea, no idea," he said, shaking his shiny, wet head. "There have been many who have entered Skull Mountain to find the Stone Key," he said sadly. "No one has ever returned."

I felt a chill go down my spine as I looked at Tim. I could tell he felt a shiver, too.

We were all still standing in the pool of water up to our necks, and it was getting kind of cold, and I said so.

"You can get out here," Otterpuss said, pointing towards a tunnel. "That will lead you back into Skull Mountain. You will be safe in the tunnel, but I must warn you . . . it is a long walk."

"Then I guess we'd better get started," Tim said, stepping out of the water. I climbed out, and Warren Otterpuss stayed in the pool.

"Good luck to you, good luck to you," he said.

"Thank you," Tim and I replied in unison.

And with that, we turned and started off through the tunnel.

The tunnel that led back into Skull Mountian.

27

Warren Otterpuss was right about the tunnel. We must have walked for miles and miles. We walked for so long that my feet started to hurt. Plus, it was really uncomfortable walking in wet clothing.

But there was one thing that was very interesting. There were no torches lit, no lights of any sort in the tunnel, but it was actually very bright just the same. After a while I realized that it was the rock walls themselves that were giving off light! It was an eerie, pink glow, giving us just enough light to see.

Soon the walls began to get wider and the ceiling above began to get higher. The tunnel was widening, and I could make out a bright glow ahead of us.

The tunnel came to an abrupt halt at an opening. We were at the opening of what looked to be a large cave that was so high in the sky it overlooked the entire island. We saw hills and trees below us, and the huge lake beyond.

I was now more certain than ever that we were somehow on Mackinac Island, only in some other time or dimension. From where we could see high above everything I recognized areas where I thought the Mackinac Bridge should be, and where the ferry docks should be. It was a really weird feeling.

"Where are we?" Tim asked, looking out at the vast expanse of the valley and forests below.

"I don't know," I answered. "We must be in Skull Mountain somewhere."

I leaned closer to the edge, looking down. A huge ledge jutted out below, sloping down like a ski hill. There was something about the ledge below me that looked familiar, something about how it jutted out . . . .

Suddenly I realized where we were!

"Tim!" I said "We're in the skull! We're in an eye of the skull!"

"Eww!" Tim said, grimacing. "We've been walking through a great big skull?!?! That's gross!"

"Well maybe so, but we've got to find that Stone Key."

"First, we have to find a way out of here," Tim said. "There is no other tunnel that leads anywhere else."

I got down on my hands and knees and looked down the ledge.

"Look!" I said excitedly. "A stone ladder! There's a stone ladder that goes down!"

And there was. A perfect ladder, carved into the stone, began at the edge of where we were. It looked like it went down the face a long, long ways.

Tim got on his hands and knees to see what I was looking at.

"Question is," he said, "Where does it lead to?"

"I don't think we have a choice at this point," I said. "There's no other way."

"It sure would be good to have that stone right now," he said.

"Well, stones or no stones, we've got to climb down." I looked up into the sky. "Come on. Let's get started before any of those ugly Wartwings show up."

Tim looked nervously up into the sky.

"All right," he said finally. "Boy . . . if Mom and Dad knew what we were doing right now, we'd be grounded for life."

"Longer than that," I added.

"I'll go first," Tim said, taking a cautious step over the ledge and onto the first stone stair.

"Be careful," I said.

Tim took another few steps down the ladder

and then I followed.

Slowly, carefully, we climbed down the face of Skull Mountain. I think if there had been anyone to see us, we would have looked like tiny ants scrambling down a huge white skull!

Finally I heard Tim shout below me.

"Hey! I reached something!" he exclaimed.

In a few more seconds I joined him on yet another ledge. I think we must have been where the skull's mouth was.

"Wow," Tim said.

All I could do was stare.

We were at the mouth of a very big cave, only this was a cave like I had never seen before. The walls were like polished glass, all shiny and bright.

And the *floor!*

The floor was made of carefully hand-laid bricks, just like the cobblestone streets of Mackinac Island.

Except—

The bricks were made of solid gold!

"Jeepers," Tim said. "It's like the Wizard of Oz or something."

"I think *that* road was made out of *yellow* brick," I corrected. "These bricks are made of *gold*."

We stared in amazement at the shiny gold floor.

"I wonder where it leads to?" Tim said.

"Only one way to find out," I said, taking a

step forward, heading for a tunnel on the far side of the cave. Tim joined me, and once again we began our journey deep into Skull Mountain.

It was very strange walking on solid gold! There must have been billions and billions of dollars in gold that we were stepping on!

"Boy, I sure would like to take a brick or two home," Tim said. "Could you imagine taking a gold brick to school for show and tell?!?!"

"If we don't find that key, we aren't going to make it home," I replied.

Suddenly the tunnel stopped at a large, silver door. The door looked heavy, and it had a large brass knob.

"You first," Tim said, stepping back from the door.

Sometimes Tim can be such a chicken.

I stepped forward and took a breath, not knowing what to expect when I opened the door. Maybe it was a trap. Maybe it was the home of some Wartwing!

Then we'd really be in trouble.

I slowly grasped the door knob and turned it. Surprisingly, it turned very easy in my hand.

The door swung open with a very loud *creeeeeaaaaakkkkk*. It seemed to take forever to open.

And I never would have imagined what we were about to see.

28

Brilliant, sparkling light. The light was so bright I couldn't see. I had to raise my arms up to shield my eyes from the intense light. So did Tim.

"What is it?" Tim whispered.

"I don't know," I said. "It's too bright. I can't see anything." The light was brighter than anything I had ever seen before.

I squinted, straining my eyes to see anything. The light appeared to be coming from something at the far end of a small room. I could make out shapes and images, but it was very hard to see.

Suddenly I saw it. The source of the light. It seemed like it was as bright as the sun . . . maybe brighter. My mouth dropped open in surprise.

The Stone Key!

"Tim!" I cried. "There it is! That's it! The Stone Key!"

"I see it!" he shouted excitedly. "I see it!"

I took a step forward into the room. The key rested in a chest on a table. It looked like it was a treasure chest. The whole room was bathed in the bright light that came from the Stone Key.

But the key didn't look like it was made out of stone. It looked like it was made out of glass. Or maybe crystal. It was big, too. As long as a pencil and as big around as a magic marker.

"Grab it and let's get out of here," Tim said.

"You bet," I said. The quicker we got out of Skull Mountain and got home to Mackinac Island, the better. I was already wondering how we were going to explain this to Mom and Dad!

I reached forward, slowly, and picked up the key.

The light went out!

As soon as I touched the key, it stopped glowing. The light faded and faded until it was gone completely.

"Geez, nice going, Sandy," Tim said. "I think you broke it."

Right. Like my brother would know.

But then something even stranger began to happen.

The key began to change in my hand!

It had been very clear and smooth, but as I

held it, it began to change. It darkened and became cloudy and discolored. Soon it was a dark, steely black.

The key had turned into stone!

"Maybe that's what the Great Tuttworth meant by the 'Stone' Key," I said. "Maybe it turns to stone if you touch it."

Tim was about to say something when he stopped short, then grabbed my arm.

"What?" I asked.

"Listen," he said. "Do you feel it?"

"Feel what?"

He held his hand up, urging me to be silent. "Listen."

Now I began to feel it. Just lightly at first, then growing. The ground began to tremble.

"Oh no!" Tim said. *"Earthquake! I think we're having an earthquake!!"*

29

The ground began to shake harder, rocking violently beneath our feet.

"Run!" I shouted, stuffing the key into my pocket and turning to bolt out the door . . . but the door was closing by itself!

"Sandy!" Tim shouted. "Hurry! The door! It's closing!"

We sprang to the door which was now almost completely closed. Tim reached it first and he thrust his hands through the small opening just in time.

"Help me pull, Sandy!" he shouted.

All around and above us the terrible quaking was growing louder and louder.

I grabbed hold of the door and pulled with everything I could. Tim lifted his leg and placed his foot on the wall to get more leverage.

It was working! The door was opening back up.

"Harder, Tim!" I yelled. The door was opening more and there was almost enough space for us to slide through.

Tim clenched his teeth, struggling as he spoke. *"Just . . . a . . . little . . . bit . . . more . . . ."*

Finally there was just enough room to escape. I slipped through first, followed quickly by Tim. The door slammed shut behind us!

We ran as fast as we could. It was hard! The ground was shaking so bad that we kept bumping into the smooth stone walls.

But we kept going. I was too scared to stop. Every so often I would stuff my hand into the pocket of my jeans, just to be sure that the key was still there.

We ran and ran, our feet pounding the gold brick floor. But we couldn't hear our footsteps over the trembling earthquake.

Small rocks and pieces of the ceiling began to fall on us. I covered my head with my hands as I ran, trying to dodge the falling debris.

"Ouch!" Tim shouted as a small rock hit him on the shoulder. "I think someone is really mad at us!"

I didn't answer. The only thing I could think of was to get out of there as quick as possible.

Finally we came to the mouth of the cave where we had come in. The gold bricks on the floor were covered with pieces of rocks that had fallen from the ceiling.

"We have to get out of here or we're done for!" I shouted above the tremendous shaking.

I climbed over the edge, searching for the stone ladder.

Please, I thought. *Oh, please be there. Please—*

My foot found something hard. I looked down along the face of the mountain and gave a sigh of relief.

The stone ladder.

I took a few steps down, holding on tight. The last thing I wanted was to fall!

"Come on!" I yelled to Tim, but he was already scrambling to the ladder.

It was tough going. The wall of the whole mountain was shaking, and small rocks were tumbling down the face. I went as fast as I dared, being careful not to lose my footing.

As we scrambled down, the blue sky above us began filling with dark storm clouds. Heavy winds began to tear at us, and it started to rain hard. Thunder rumbled, and soon lightning bolts were streaking across the sky. One struck the rock wall very close to us! The thunderous boom echoed over the island.

"We have to hurry!" Tim screamed from above me.

"I'm going as fast as I can!" I shouted back.

The entire mountain was trembling harder and harder. Large pieces of rock were thundering by, bouncing off the side of the mountain and tumbling and spinning to the ground far below.

But we *were* getting closer. When I looked down I could make out trees and large rocks and even a pond.

The stone ladder, wet with rain, became very slippery. It was getting harder and harder to hold on! It was also even harder because I had to keep looking up to make sure I would get out of the way of any large rocks that were falling.

I looked back down.

We were at treetop level! Just a little bit farther . . . .

A small rock bounced off my back and I looked back up.

Oh no!

I was horrified by what I saw.

"TIM!!" I screamed. *"TIM!!! LOOK OUT!!"*

It was a boulder . . . a HUGE one . . . and it was going to come down right on top of us!

30

Tim heard my scream and he looked up.

"Aaaagghhh!!" he screamed. He ducked in close to the side of the mountain, holding the ladder with all of his strength. There was nowhere he could go!

I couldn't go anywhere either. I could only watch, helpless, as the enormous rock hurled down right toward us.

Suddenly there was an enormous boom. I thought lightning had struck again.

But it was the boulder! It had hit the face of the mountain right above Tim! It struck hard enough to cause it to re-direct, and it bounced out a few feet and tumbled right over us!

That was a close one. The rock was the size

of a truck. If it would have hit us, we would have been crushed!

"I think this is our lucky day, Munchkin!" Tim shouted from above.

"It's not going to be lucky for you if you keep calling me Munchkin!" I shouted back. And I meant it.

We kept climbing down, step by step, as the storm battered us. It was raining so hard I couldn't see, and the wind almost pushed me off the stone ladder. Rocks and stones continued falling. I knew that at any minute the mountain was going to come crashing down on us.

Suddenly I was on the ground! I made it!

Tim was only a few feet above me and he jumped.

"Let's get out of here!" he shouted, running towards a clump of trees.

I followed him but it was hard. The trembling ground made running awkward. But we didn't stop until we were far from the mountain. Finally, we were far enough away that the quaking wasn't so bad.

I stopped running and so did Tim. We were panting and out of breath.

And the rain had stopped! It had been pouring just a few minutes ago, but now there wasn't a single drop falling from the sky. I hadn't noticed it before, but the sky had turned blue and the sun was shining.

"Wow," Tim said, pointing. "Look at that!"

I turned to see what he was looking at. Tim was staring off over the treetops, looking at Skull Mountain.

The entire mountain was collapsing! We could hear the rumbling from where we stood, and I watched in disbelief as the whole face of the skull crumbled and broke away! Lightning bolts continued to blaze through the sky above the mountain, and dark clouds hovered over it. The mountain continued to fall apart, piece by piece.

I sure was glad we made it out of there!

But I wasn't real happy with what I was about to see.

"Tim?" I stammered. "What's . . . what's that big cloud coming toward us?"

Tim looked in the direction of where I was pointing my finger. He didn't say a thing.

He didn't need to. I knew what the cloud was. It seemed to be boiling, churning about, speeding through the air.

Wartwings.

Not two, not three.

Hundreds of them.

Thousands of them.

And they were coming right for us!

31

I couldn't believe what I was seeing! The giant Wartwings were out in full force, swooping through the sky and coming right toward us.

And something told me that they were *mad*.

"Come on!" Tim shouted. He sprang and started to run. I followed, but I wasn't sure if this was such a good idea.

As we ran, I kept glancing up into the sky to see the Wartwings. They were getting closer.

I ran, following Tim as he sped through the forest. We ran and ran as fast as our legs could take us, through swamps and over rocks. Over a small stream and over fallen trees. We continued running, faster, faster still . . . .

Until we came to the River of Dreams.

"Oh, man!" Tim said, smacking his head with the palm of his hand. "I forgot about the river! I forgot about the River of Dreams!"

"We have to find the tree that we came over on!" I shouted frantically.

"But which way do we go?" Tim asked. "Upstream or downstream?"

Call it a hunch or whatever, but I thought that we should go downstream, and I told Tim that.

"Let's go!" he shouted, and suddenly we were running again. I turned to see the cloud of Wartwings in the distance, still coming our way, getting closer with every passing second.

My hunch was right on. After about five minutes, we came to the tree that crossed the river. Tim laid down on the fallen trunk and I climbed onto his back, clinging tightly around his neck.

"Now remember," I warned. "Don't look down. Whatever you do, don't look down."

"Geesh, you don't have to tell me," Tim said.

Tim began to crawl steadily across the fallen tree. To make sure I didn't look into the dark waters below, I turned my head up and stared at the sky.

Behind us, the Wartwings were coming full force. I could see their wings flapping in the sky, thousands of them, all coming toward us.

"Hurry, Tim, hurry," I said. But he was already going pretty fast.

Finally, we made it across. I climbed off Tim

and we both bounded to our feet, running once again. I have never ran so much. Ever.

I heard a loud cry and turned around, and I was instantly terrified.

The Wartwings had caught up with us!

They were only a hundred feet away, snarling viciously above the treetops. I could hear them squealing with delight as they came closer. I could even hear their huge wings beating the air. They were the ugliest, meanest looking things I had ever seen in my life.

"*TIM!*" I screamed. *"Tim, they're almost here!"*

Tim turned just long enough to see the swarming Wartwings. They were everywhere. Crashing through the trees, swooping out of the sky like eagles.

"Keep running!" Tim shouted. "I think I see a cave up ahead!"

I hoped he was right.

Suddenly Tim ducked down, climbing on his hands and knees.

It was a cave! The opening was small, but it was a cave all right!

I fell to my hands and knees and struggled to get into the small opening. I could see Tim crawling in front of me.

Suddenly, I felt something grab my leg! It snapped me backwards and began to pull.

A Wartwing!

I hadn't quite made it all the way through the small opening, and one of the Wartwings had grabbed me with its claw!

"TIM!! HELP!!! HELP MEEEEE!!!!"

32

The Wartwing began to drag me back out, but Tim grabbed my hand and began pulling me back in. I kicked as hard as I could but it was no use. The Wartwing was too strong.

"Don't let go, Tim!" I screamed.

"I can't hold on!" he shouted back. "I'm trying . . . but I can't hold on!"

And suddenly he couldn't. Tim tried, but the furious grip of the Wartwing was too strong. I felt him lose his grip and his hands slipped away.

I was pulled back out, kicking and screaming at the top of my lungs. Dozens of Wartwings were swarming all around now, some landing on the ground, some hovering in the air above.

"LET ME GO!" I yelled, but the Wartwing

held fast. It was horrible looking. The creature had huge, diamond-shaped eyes that were as black as night. Its mouth was huge, and I could see rows and rows of fangs the size of steak knives.

This was it. I'm a goner.

Then, above the screeching of the Wartwings, I heard another sound.

Barking! It was the barking of dogs! Lots and lots of dogs! I could hear them yelping and snarling. The bulldogs had come to my rescue!

The barking distracted some of the Wartwings and they turned their attention away from me. I could see dogs running all over the place now, viciously snarling and snapping at the Wartwings. The bulldogs were everywhere. They were using their horns to poke at the Wartwings. Some of the winged creatures took flight, others stayed on the ground, trying to fend off the ferocious attacking dogs.

Then I recognized Bart! He came zipping through the madness, barking and snarling at the Wartwing that still held my foot. He seized a wing and pulled, and the Wartwing let out a screech . . . and let go.

I was free!

"Hurry!" Bart the bulldog barked. "Get back inside the cave!"

He didn't have to tell me twice!

I spun and climbed through the small opening,

and Tim and I watched from the safety of the small doorway.

Hundreds of bulldogs continued to bark and growl at the Wartwings. They circled the creatures, baring their teeth and snapping into the air. These dogs meant business!

The sheer number of dogs and their ferociousness were too much for the Wartwings. Disgusted, they took flight, beating the air with their wings and screeching in anger. Soon only the dogs were left.

Bart sauntered up to the opening of the cave. Tim and I backed away so he could come in.

"Thank you!" I said, and threw my arms around the dog. He thumped his tail happily.

"It was an honor and a pleasure," the bulldog said. "The news traveled fast. When we heard that you had found the Stone Key but were in trouble, the alarm went out all over the Isle of Mayhem. You're lucky you found the back door to my home."

Back door! How lucky could we get in one day?

"But . . . how did you know we found the key?" Tim asked. I was puzzled, too.

"The destruction of Skull Mountain," Bart answered. "But please. Let's go inside and I'll explain further."

With the bulldog leading the way, Tim and I crawled on our hands and knees and followed the dog into his home. Taking a seat on the floor near a bowl of water, Bart began.

"When we heard the earthquake and saw Skull Mountain begin to collapse, we knew you had found the Stone Key. All of the dark forces of the Isle of Mayhem welled up to try and stop you. That's why the Wartwings were after you. They brought out their entire army . . . every last one. Because they knew if you escaped, they would be cast into the Abyss of No Return."

"And you came and saved me," I said. "You saved us!"

The bulldog nodded. "We, as a pack, had to do everything we could to help you make it to safety. All of us want to see the Isle of Miracles return. Now, thanks to you, that is possible. But enough for now. You must be very tired. Get some sleep and I'll tell you more in the morning. You have a big day ahead of you. We still have to get you to the Captive Forest . . . and that might not be very easy."

33

The next thing I knew I was on the floor and Bart was nuzzling me with his nose.

"Good morning, sleepyhead," he said. "You slept a long time." But it really didn't feel like I had slept at all.

Tim was already awake and he was sitting up. His hair went every which-way. Bed-head, that's what I call it. He looked funny. But I'm sure my hair didn't look much better.

"Oh, I almost forgot," Bart the bulldog said. "I have something for both of you."

The bulldog, tail wagging, bounded to a table and picked up two small objects in his mouth, and brought them to us.

Our stones!

"They must have fallen from your pockets the last time you were here," the dog said. "I found them on the floor after you left."

I took the two stones and gave the one with the spider on it to Tim. He looked at it for a moment and then shoved it into his pocket. I did the same with mine.

"Come," he said. "Let's go and unlock the Captive Forest. All of the island creatures have been waiting for this day."

The walk to the other side of the island took us a long time. We walked and walked and walked. We were joined by lots and lots of other bulldogs. They all came to help make sure we would make it back safely.

Bart talked the whole time. He told us all about the Isle and the evil King Balderdash, and how he had taken over the island. He told us about the Abyss of No Return, which was an invisible dark hole way on the other side of the island.

"When you unlock the Captive Forest," the dog said, "all of the evil creatures will be consumed by the Abyss. The Isle of Mayhem will be no more. It will return to the Isle of Miracles."

"Where we come from," I said, "we call this Mackinac Island. There are people and houses and animals, but not like what you have here."

Bart seemed amused.

"I would like to see that island some day," he

said.

I was happy. I knew Tim was happy. Soon we would be unlocking the Captive Forest. Soon the Great Tuttworth would be free.

Soon we could go home.

Unfortunately, it wasn't going to be that easy.

We hadn't counted on the Blinkmongers.

34

They attacked from out of nowhere. Huge, ape-like creatures with gigantic eyes. Eyes that blinked constantly. I guess that's why they called them Blinkmongers.

"Run!" Bart shouted to us. "Run ahead and we'll try to keep them back! You're only a few hundred feet from the Captive Forest!"

Tim and I did as we were instructed, running as fast as we could. The Blinkmongers were everywhere . . . hanging from branches, sitting in trees, running all over the place. When they saw us, they took up chase.

They were kind of slow . . . much slower than the speedy Wartwings, and certainly a lot slower than the dogs that accompanied us.

But there were so *many* of them. Hundreds and hundreds of them. I thought we might be able to outrun them, but soon we were surrounded. Tim and I were in the center, ringed by a dozen dogs that were protecting us. Around the ring of dogs was a bigger ring.

A ring of Blinkmongers.

They grunted and groaned and made horrible growling noises. It was awful. There must have been hundreds of them.

The dogs around us kept snarling and snapping at them, trying to keep the Blinkmongers away from us. Bart came to my side.

"Use your stones," he whispered. "You can use your stones to get away. If you can make it to the Captive Forest, you'll be safe. The Blinkmongers can't go into the Captive Forest."

"What do they want with us?" Tim asked.

"Oh, I'm sure they think that you'll be quite delicious," Bart replied.

Gulp.

"But what about you?" I asked. "What will happen to you?" I truly didn't want anything to happen to my new friend.

"I'll be fine. It's not us they want. It's *you*. It's the Stone Key. They know that once you unlock the captive forest, they'll be thrown into the Abyss of No Return."

But how could it work, I wondered. I could

use my stone to fly, but Tim could only use his to crawl like a spider.

Then I had an idea. I didn't know if it would work or not, but right now it was the only hope I had.

"Tim," I said. "Put your arms around me and hang on."

"Huh?" he said. "You mean give you a hug?"

"Yes! Just do it!" I whispered loudly. "It's our only chance."

He put his arms around me, and I put my arms around him.

"Now . . . *hold on tight!*"

Suddenly we were flying! It was working! We sailed up into the air, not very high, but high enough to be out of reach of those ugly Blinkmongers.

"It's working!" Tim shouted. He was laughing, and then I started laughing, too! It was really working!

"Good-bye!" I shouted to the dogs as we drifted farther and farther away. "Good-bye and thank you!"

I could see the Captive Forest getting closer, and the group of Blinkmongers getting smaller. We drew closer and closer, but soon we began to slowly fall. I remembered what the Great Tuttworth had said about the power of flying, and that it would wear out quickly.

Not wanting to take any chances, we settled

safely back on the ground right next to the Captive Forest. Behind us, the Blinkmongers were coming, but they were a long ways away. Much too far to be able to catch us before we entered the forest.

"Ready?" I asked Tim.

"You bet," he said.

We stepped into the Captive Forest.

35

It wasn't hard to find the Great Tuttworth. He was sitting in a large tree, waiting for us! I could see his white robe and pointy hat.

"We've got the Stone Key!" Tim shouted.

"I know, I know!" the Great Tuttworth shouted. "All of the creatures of the Captive Forest have told me! This is the happiest day of my life!"

He came down from the tree and ran toward us! Although he seemed like a very old man, he was really very agile and strong.

I pulled the Stone Key from my pocket and held it out. He took it slowly, gazing at it like a child, holding it up to see.

"The Stone Key," he said. "Finally. Now I can be free. Now we can return the Isle to its rightful condition."

And with that he turned and began walking away.

"Mr. Tuttworth?" I called out. "Sir? How do we get home?"

But he didn't answer! He just kept walking, so we had no choice but to follow him. He walked along a path and over a hill and soon we were deep into the forest.

He stopped in front of a strange door. When we drew closer, we realized that it wasn't a door at all, but a wall of water! It was the size of a door, but it looked to be completely made out of water. It rippled and I could see small waves on its surface.

"The Door of Realms," the Great Tuttworth said. He was speaking very slowly, smiling. "Now, all things can be right again."

And with that, he placed the key against the shimmering surface of water.

What happened next was nothing less than spectacular! The door changed colors, glowing brighter, then darker, then brighter again. It was breathtaking. The colors of everything around us began to change. Purples, yellows, blues, reds and greens. Tim and I watched, awestruck by the incredible scene before us.

Then the flashing colors stopped. The door returned to its normal, transparent texture. There was a great whooshing sound, like the sound of a jet flying overhead as the Captive Forest was unlocked, held captive no more.

"It has been a long time," the Great Tuttworth said, smiling. "I cannot thank you enough. The spell is broken and the Isle of Miracles is once again."

I looked around. It sure didn't look like much had changed.

"But everything looks the same," Tim said, his eyes scanning the sky and the trees.

"Ah, yes, it does," the Great Tuttworth replied. "Here in the forest, nothing would have changed, except it is now no longer the 'Captive' Forest. All around the island, things have changed back to the way they should be. But now for your situation. You must be very ready to go home."

"We sure are," I said. "What do we do?"

He turned and looked at the strange door. "You must enter the Door of Realms," he said.

Both Tim and I were quiet for a few moments, staring at the strange, rippling door.

"What is going to happen?" Tim asked.

I have to admit, even I was curious as to how we were going to use the door to get back to Mackinac Island.

But then again, after what I had just been through, I would believe just about anything!

"The Door of Realms will take you to the world that you came from. You will not be hurt. Are you ready?"

Suddenly I felt very sad. Sure I wanted to go home, but I also was going to miss my new friends here on the Isle of Mayhem . . . which was now the Isle of Miracles. I was going to miss funny Warren Otterpuss and Bart the bulldog and even the Great Tuttworth, even though he was the one responsible for us being here in the first place.

But I sure wouldn't miss the Wartwings and the Blinkmongers or Skull Mountain! And you can bet that there were no giant sea snakes on Mackinac Island, either.

"Will we ever see you again?" I asked.

The Great Miracle-Maker shook his head. "Your job is done," he said. "And a fine, fine job you both did. The Isle of Miracles will forever be grateful to you for finding the Stone Key. But no . . . after you leave, you will not return. However, the Isle of Miracles will always be here, just as your Mackinac Island will always be. I wish you both well."

Tim stepped forward and extended his hand. The Great Tuttworth took it. It was both a handshake of friendship and a handshake of good-bye.

"See you later," Tim said.

The Miracle-Maker looked at him with a puzzled expression. "You will?" he asked.

"Well, not really," Tim said. "It's just an expression. It means 'good-bye' . . . but I guess you're right. I won't be seeing you later."

The Great Tuttworth turned to me and I threw my arms around him and gave him a big hug.

"Good-bye," I said, pulling away.

"Good-bye, my new friends. Good-bye. May all your dreams come true."

Reluctantly, Tim and I both stepped closer to the shimmering wall of water. After a moment of hesitation, we walked into the strange, liquid-like door.

36

Everything was really fuzzy. When I opened my eyes, the sun was shining. I was laying on the ground in the woods, and the old, dead tree loomed over me. I could hear birds and crickets and a plane buzzing overhead. I propped myself up on my elbows.

I was home! It was Mackinac Island! Through the trees I could still see my bicycle propped up against a tree by the lake. Tim lay on the ground next to me.

"Tim!" I said, shaking him. "Tim . . . we're back! We're on Mackinac Island again!"

Tim opened his eyes and looked disoriented. Then he sat up, looking around. Suddenly he realized that we made it back safely.

"Mom and Dad!" he exclaimed. "We have to get home! Boy, are we going to be in trouble! We've been gone for days!!"

He leapt to his feet and I did the same, crashing through the brush.

We literally *flew* home on our bikes. I pedaled as fast as I could. We wound down through Main street, past horses and people and other bicyclists. Finally we made it to our house.

Tim was the first off his bike and he leaned it against the wood fence and tore up the sidewalk. I was close behind!

"Mom! Dad! Here we are! We're home!" Tim shouted as he opened the door and burst into the house. I was right on his heels as we flew through the living room and into the kitchen. Mom was preparing dinner with Aunt Ruth.

"Oh, I'm so glad," Mom said. "I need you both to run to the grocery store and pick up some things."

Huh?

Did I just hear what I think I heard?

"But Mom," I said. "We're home! We're finally home!"

"Yes, dear, I can see that. But I really need your help. Your Aunt Ruth and I can't leave while we're cooking, and your father and your uncle are out fishing. Could you please go to the market?"

Tim and I just stared at each other. We *must*

have been gone for two or three days . . . but Mom acted like we had only been gone for a bike ride!

"Uh . . . sure Mom," I said. She handed me some money and a list of grocery items.

"Hurry back," she said.

Tim and I left quietly, not speaking until we were outside.

"She's not mad at all," he said. He couldn't believe it, either.

"Maybe . . . maybe the whole thing didn't happen," I said, climbing on my bicycle.

"But that's impossible, Sandy. We couldn't have dreamed it. That would mean that you and I had the exact same dream!"

Tim was right. It was impossible that we could have imagined or dreamed what we had been through. But there was no other explanation. The entire time we had spent on the Isle of Mayhem must not have taken up any time on Mackinac Island. We must have been in some sort of strange time warp, and while we were away, time had stopped. Or, at the very least, slowed down a whole lot.

We returned from the grocery store and gave the bag to Mom.

"Mom," I said. "How long were we gone? I mean . . . when we rode around the island?" I had to know.

Mom scrunched her eyebrows together and then glanced up at the clock on the wall.

"Oh, an hour maybe. Actually, I was surprised to see you both so soon. I didn't expect you to return so quickly."

Weird. Just plain weird.

37

Later that night we had dinner and then Dad surprised us with a bonfire by the lake. We roasted marshmallows and made S'mores. They were delicious!

The next day when I woke up, Mom was already awake when I stumbled groggily into the kitchen. She was putting glasses in the cupboard.

"Good morning," she said.

"G'mornin'," I said sleepily.

I poured myself a glass of orange juice and sat down at the table. I thought long and hard about all of the things that had happened yesterday. The Isle of Mayhem, the Miracle-Maker, Warren Otterpuss, the Wartwings. And the kind bulldog that saved us from certain death. It just didn't make sense.

Could it all have been a dream?

Was it possible? Did Tim and I fall asleep and have the same dream?

"Oh . . . I washed your jeans last night after you went to bed," Mom said, walking towards the table. "I found these. They must have been in your pockets. They made an awful racket in the dryer." She held out her hand.

In her palm were two stones. One had a dragonfly carved into it, and the other had a spider.

Just then, I remembered the last words the Great Tuttworth had told us.

'May all your dreams come true,' he had said.

May all you dreams come true.

I took the stones from Mom's hand. "Thanks," I said. "We, uh . . . we bought them at a gift shop."

"I thought you'd want them back," Mom said. "What do they mean?"

Lost for an answer, I simply said that they were called 'dream stones'. There was no way I could tell her what had really happened! I mean . . . come on. Could I really expect Mom to believe that we had been on the Isle of Mayhem, and that we had battled Blinkmongers and Wartwings and Skull Mountain? Mom would think I'd gone bonkers!

"Well, sweetheart," she said, kissing me on the forehead. "May all your dreams come true."

38

I stayed outside most of the day. Tim had gone fishing with Dad, and I was waiting for my friend Matt Sorenson. Matt and his family are from Traverse City and every summer they spend a week on Mackinac Island. I met him a couple years ago. He's really cool and we have a lot of fun.

I haven't seen Matt since last summer. Today he was going to come over and we were going to walk downtown and hang out. It was a sunny, warm day. A perfect day on Mackinac Island.

Soon I saw him walking up the street. Matt is a little bit taller than me. He looked the same as last year . . . same dark brown hair. Same walk. He had on a pair of shorts and a blue t-shirt.

"Hi Matt!" I said.

"Hey San," he said. That's what he calls me. San. I don't think he's ever called me 'Sandy'. Always 'San'.

At least he doesn't call me Munchkin!

"Wait till I tell you what happened to my brother and I yesterday!" I said.

"Me first," he replied quickly. "Because *you're* not going to believe what happened to *me* last Christmas in Traverse City . . . ."

Next in the
'Michigan Chillers'
series!

#2 : Terror Stalks
Traverse City

Go to the next page for a few
sample chapters!

Ever since I can remember, I've always wanted to be a magician. You know the kind...like the ones you see on TV that can make animals disappear and saw people in half. Well, not really saw them in half, but they sure make it look like they do! Once on TV, I saw a magician make a whole plane disappear. I know it was only a trick, but it sure was cool.

But last Christmas one of my presents was a magic kit . . . and let me tell you, it changed my mind *completely* about wanting to be a magician!

The problem started a couple days before Christmas. I was upstairs in my bedroom and my sister was downstairs watching TV.

"Matt!" my dad hollered up to me. "A package came for you in the mail today! You too,

Kimmy!"

A package? For me? Cool! I hardly ever get mail!

"Ohboyohboyohboy!" I heard my sister say from downstairs. She's six years old and gets excited about anything. I'm eleven, so I've been around the block a few more times than her.

But I was still excited to get something in the mail!

I ran downstairs to find two large brown packages on the kitchen table. Kimmy was already there, her eyes all bugged out at the sight of a box waiting for her and her alone.

"I think they're from Grandma and Grandpa," Dad said.

I picked up the package and read the address label.

Mr. Matthew Sorenson
2456 Willow Street
Traverse City, MI 49685

But right below the label was a note that got me really excited:

Do NOT wait till Christmas! Open immediately!

Cool!

"Can I open mine, Daddy?" Kimmy asked.

"Well, the note says not to wait," Dad said. "So I guess you'd better open it right away."

I didn't even ask Dad if I could open mine! I knew already that I was supposed to open it.

I couldn't wait. Grandma and Grandpa always get me the coolest stuff. Last year grandpa got me a model rocket that really worked! This year . . . well, who knows?

I cut the packaging tape with a pair of scissors and opened the box. Inside was a card addressed to me, and a bunch of popcorn. You know the kind of popcorn I'm talking about . . . those little white puffy kernels made of foam. They keep whatever is inside the box from shifting around and getting damaged.

I shuffled through the popcorn with my hands and found still another package. This one was wrapped in blue and gold Christmas wrapping paper. A silver bow was attached to the top of it.

Kimmy had already opened up her package and was tearing off the wrapping paper on her gift. She had spilled white foam popcorn all over the floor.

"It's a Barbie!" she suddenly yelled.

"Do you have to be so loud?" I said. Kimmy has this really high-pitched voice. She can be so annoying sometimes. She just stuck out her tongue at me. Typical sister.

I began tearing into the wrapping paper. What

was it going to be this year? A model airplane? Maybe a super giant ant farm! That would be neat.

But when I tore away the final layer of wrapping paper, I just stared.

"Wow," I whispered.

I couldn't believe what I was seeing.

2

I read the big block letters out loud:

"PROFESSIONAL STAGE MAGICIAN KIT," it read. Right beneath that: "Over 100 magic tricks included!"

"Wow!" I said again, only this time I didn't whisper.

A magic kit! I had always wanted one! How did Grandma and Grandpa know?

"Lemmee see! Lemmee see!" Kimmy shouted.

"Go on, go play with your doll," I said, turning away from her. For once, she listened to me. She picked up her Barbie and went into the living room.

I looked at the box, reading the words again. This was going to be fun!

My own magic kit. Card tricks, disappearing tricks . . . it was all there.

My very own magic kit.

I couldn't wait. I had to go learn some magic right now. Then I could show everyone some magic tricks for Christmas! Uncle Dave and Aunt Kate would be coming, and of course my twin cousins, Alex and Adrian. Maybe I could even put on a magic show!

But I'd have to get started. Christmas was only three days away. That didn't give me much time to learn a lot of magic tricks.

I took the box upstairs to my room and opened it up. I spread out the contents all over my bed. There was a manual, a hat, a cape, and all kinds of cool stuff.

This was going to be a great Christmas! The best ever.

Now, looking back, I wish I'd NEVER opened up that box. I didn't know it at the time, but what was about to happen almost wrecked Christmas—not only for me, but for the whole city!

3

Maybe I could have prevented any problems if I would have read the manual first. But I was in such a hurry to get started that I began playing around with the things that were included in the magic kit. I never even gave the manual a second glance.

Not yet, anyway.

I shuffled through a deck of trick cards. I found a small plastic tube that was supposed to make a penny disappear. There was also a small box that had a secret opening in the bottom to make it look like whatever was placed in the box would vanish.

Then I found the magic wand.

It looked just like you would expect a magic

wand to look like. It was about as long as my arm and all black, except for a white tip. Very cool.

Just then I heard banging on my door.

"Matt!" I heard Kimmy say. "Matt! I wanna see your magic kit!"

"Go away," I said. "I'm learning how to do magic."

"But I wanna see!" she persisted. Sometimes she can be such a pest.

"All right," I said. "But when I open up this door, I'm going to make you disappear."

That did the trick. I heard her footsteps running away from the door and back downstairs.

"Dad!" I heard her shout. "Daddy . . . Matt is going to make me disappear! Don't let him, Daddy!"

Sisters.

I experimented with the cards for a few minutes. It looked like an ordinary deck, except there were a couple special cards. There was even a card that shot water like a water pistol! That would be fun.

There was also a small tray that turned a one dollar bill into a five dollar bill. That would be even MORE fun!

And a black hat. It was a real magician's hat, one that you wore on your head and pulled rabbits out of.

Well, I guess I kind of figured you could pull rabbits out of it. There certainly weren't any rabbits included with the kit.

I plopped the hat onto my head and looked into the mirror.

"Hey," I said to myself. "That looks good." I really did look like a magician. My black hair stuck out from the sides of the hat. I'm taller than most kids my age, and a little thinner, too. The hat made me look even taller. I think I might have looked like a young Abraham Lincoln, except he had a really big nose. I don't.

I rummaged through the stuff on my bed and found another part of the magician's uniform . . . a long black cape.

I draped it over my shoulders and looked into the mirror again.

That looked even better. Wow! Was this going to be a cool Christmas! I was going to do magic tricks for everyone on Christmas day.

But my outfit wasn't complete yet. All I needed to *really* look like a magician was—

The magic wand.

I picked it up and looked into the mirror.

"That's cool," I whispered. I really *did* look like a magician.

I held the wand up, and waved it back and forth, pretending to make something disappear. I thought it would be really fun if I could make something vanish.

Little did I know I was about to make

something *really* disappear.
And that's when the trouble began.

4

On my wall I have a paper drawing that I made in school. It was a drawing of lots of Christmas things—a snowman, a bunch of elves, Santa's reindeer, and a snow monster. The snow monster looked creepy. I gave him big red eyes and long fangs and white hair all over his body. The elves were all different colors and had pointed hats with a little dingle-ball on top. Their chins were pointy and so were their noses.

I decided that I would make the poster disappear.

"Allakazzaam!" I shouted as I waved the wand in the air. As I spoke, I pointed the wand at the poster.

The poster stayed right where it was, taped to the wall.

Hmmm. That didn't work. I wondered what else I could try.

I looked around the room, and something outside my window caught my attention. I walked over to the window and peered down at the snow-covered yard below.

It was getting dark, but there was still enough light to see pretty well.

And what I saw made my eyes go wide and my jaw drop.

There were tiny elves running all over the yard! And reindeer! Even a snowman was walking around!

I rubbed my eyes, not believing what I was seeing.

But it was real! I could see them as clear as anything.

That's when I suddenly realized something, and I turned around in shock, afraid of what I would see.

The poster.

The paper was still on the wall, but all of my drawings—the elves, the reindeer, the snowman—all of them were missing! They were no longer on the paper!

I turned around again and looked down into the yard.

The elves were running about all over the place, and the reindeer were too. They had even gone into our neighbor's yard . . . and boy, had they started to cause problems! The elves were climbing up trees that had been decorated. They were pulling off the lights and throwing them into the snow. I could see them smiling and laughing at their own mischievousness.

"Hey!" I yelled at them through the window. "Hey! You can't do that!"

I didn't think they could hear me, but one of the elves that had climbed up a Christmas tree looked up.

He stuck his tongue out at me!

This was not good. This was not good at all.

The reindeer had gotten into my mom's flower garden. Obviously there were no flowers, just snow—but the reindeer pawed at the ground and dug up dirt! They left big holes in the garden! Mom's gonna freak!

I still couldn't believe what I was seeing. The creatures in my drawing had actually come to life. They were scurrying about all over the yard and into the street.

Suddenly, one of the elves climbed the light post in front of our house. The post was decorated with lights and tinsel and garland.

Do you know what that little stinker did? He pulled everything off! And I mean everything! He yanked off the colorful Christmas lights and they all blinked out. He pulled down the tinsel and garland, slid down the post, and stomped all over the decorations! They were going to destroy the whole yard!

Suddenly I shivered, and I turned and looked back at the blank poster on the wall.

If the elves had come alive . . . .

And the reindeer were alive, too . . . .

And if the snowman had come alive . . . .

Then that would mean . . . .

I shuddered at the thought.

The snow monster.

He was alive, too!

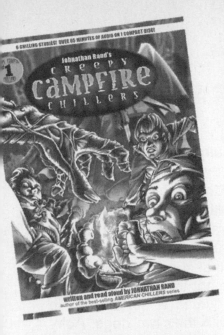

About the author

Johnathan Rand is the author of the best-selling **'Chillers'** series, now with over 2,000,000 copies in print. In addition to the **'Chillers'** series, Rand is also the author of the **'Adventure Club'** series, including **'Ghost in the Graveyard', 'Ghost in the Grand',** and **'The Haunted Schoolhouse',** three collections of thrilling, original short stories. When Mr. Rand and his wife are not traveling to schools and book signings, they live in a small town in northern lower Michigan with their two dogs, Abby and Lily Munster. He is currently working on more 'Chillers', as well as a new series for younger readers entitled **'Freddie Fernortner, Fearless First Grader'.** His popular website features hundreds of photographs, stories, and art work. Visit:

www.americanchillers.com

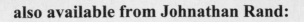

Join the official

AMERICAN CHILLERS

FAN CLUB!

Visit www.americanchillers.com for details

All AudioCraft books are proudly printed, bound, and manufactured in the United States of America, utilizing American resources, labor, and materials.

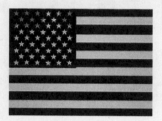

USA